Can't Get Here from There:
Fifty Tales of Travel

by
Jeremiah A. Gilbert

Copyright© 2020 Jeremiah A. Gilbert
ISBN: 978-93-90202-78-2

First Edition: 2020
Rs. 200/-

Cyberwit.net
HIG 45 Kaushambi Kunj, Kalindipuram
Allahabad - 211011 (U.P.) India
http://www.cyberwit.net
Tel: +(91) 9415091004 +(91) (532) 2552257
E-mail: info@cyberwit.net

Printed at Repro India Limited.

For A.J.G. and J.E.G.

Introduction

California – Fall 2020

My father was not a traveler. For one, he feared flying, meaning that the few vacations we took in my youth were long crawls across many states in whatever second-hand car we owned at the time. He also didn't like to spend money, so we'd stay in whichever motel was vacant and cheapest, and pack in as many miles as possible the next day as that meant fewer motels. I recall one particularly cheap motel in Houston. We'd been driving all day and arrived late, so we all went straight to sleep. The next morning, in the light of day, we noticed the swarm of cockroaches in the bathtub and made a quick departure. My father was determined that he didn't want to spend another night in Texas, which meant another long driving day as we were heading west along Interstate 10. My mother and I agreed, on the condition that we chose that night's accommodation.

I assume this contributed to my being a late bloomer when it comes to travel. That and the fact that one doesn't make much on an adjunct professor's salary. I started teaching straight out of grad school. In order to make ends meet, I had a certain number of classes I had to teach, which meant teaching at multiple colleges, and always teaching summers. I did this for several years before landing a full-time teaching position, which I still hold. Suddenly my health insurance was paid for and my summer teaching was optional.

Where to first? Tibet, of course, where I was able to spend my thirty-fifth birthday on the Great Wall before flying from Beijing to Lhasa and exploring the Potala Palace. I'd heard the train through Mexico's Copper Canyon was quite an experience, so that was next. This was followed by Peru as I've always had a love of ruins and lost cities, and Machu Picchu doesn't disappoint. Once I'd reached five countries, ten didn't seem out of reach. After ten, twenty, and after twenty, fifty.

Fortunately, when I'd meet the woman who would become my wife in Tunisia, she was also an avid traveler. In fact, after we started planning trips together, I asked her to make a list of everywhere she'd been and which countries she'd be willing to return to. She did, with the caveat that she always remain one country ahead of me. I've kept that promise for over a decade, though do try to talk her out of it every so often.

The follow travel tales are chronological and do not cover everywhere I've been. I've tried to focus on memorable occasions and interesting occurrences, though there are many more tales to be told. I've included fifty of them as I turn fifty next year, so that number has been on my mind a lot lately. As of this writing, the country count sits at eighty-five (eighty-six for my wife), though the coronavirus has put a stop to the count for now. We had planned a trip to Fiji and New Zealand in April and a return to Peru in June, but both were sidelined. I don't image traveling out of the country again until next year. But, as this year has proven, stranger things have happened.

J.A.G.

Contents

Two Bowls for the Price of One 9

Beijing Taxi Tales 11

El Gringo Loco 15

My Man in Cusco 17

A Disappointing Drawbridge 19

Araceli's Flower 21

Into the Yukon with Mopps 23

Birthday Impromptu 25

Trying to Avoid a Stoning in Fez 27

The Wandering Wallet 29

Silver and Bones 31

Lost in Transit: Arriving 33

Lost in Transit: Departing 37

A Disputed Territory (and Guidebook) 39

Form over Function 41

Camel-Jacked 43

Night Train to Luxor 45

Ashes to Ashes 47

Two for Ten Thouuuuuusaaaaaand! 49

Paris Metro Pros and Cons 51

For the Want of Cold Water 55

Stranger on a Train 57

Pyongyang via Phnom Penh 59

Bhat-less in Bangkok 61

It's Not the End of the World as We Know It 63

A Good Night's Sleep 65

Really Putting My Foot in It 67

Fogged Up in Cartagena 69

Yes, We Have It, but It Doesn't Work 71

Don't Worry, There is No Flesh 73

Checkpoint Smuggling 75

Monkey Versus Monkey 77

Irish Karma 79

Seven-Star High Tea 81
Christmas in Qatar 83
Grounded by Air Force One 85
Not So Happy Birthday to Me 87
Never Judge a Church by Its Exterior 89
Art Underground 91
Roaming in Rome 93
Museo a Cielo Abierto 95
An Unwelcoming Welcome 97
A Second Honeymoon 99
Delta Glamping 101
A Slow Crossing 103
Here Staircase, Staircase 105
Losing My Seat in London 107
The Picky Eater 109
A Non-Inclusive Tour 111
Can't Get Here from There 113

Two Bowls for the Price of One

Tibet – July 2006

I am not a very good haggler. My general approach is quite simple: After asking for the price, if it is good, I buy; if it's too high, I walk away. This often leads to the seller haggling on my behalf until the price drops low enough for me to buy. It's not sophisticated, but it has served me well. Though I do need to be able to walk away for this method to work.

Lhasa's Barkhor is a public square and area of narrow streets located around Jokhang Temple. I've got an hour to kill before attending a chanting ceremony in the temple, so I wander about the stalls that line the narrow streets. In my wandering, I make a wrong turn in search of something cold to drink and end up down a very aggressive lane. I notice a man sitting in the middle of the road and, as I approach, he greets me and reaches out his hand. I greet him in return and shake his hand. Without letting go of my hand, I am led to his stall where he wants to know what I'd like to buy.

Seeing I am looking about for an exit, his grip tightens while another vendor comes up and holds my opposite shoulder. I've never been held in place while shopping before and figure I'm going to need to buy something to get out of this situation. I notice a singing bowl that I quite like and ask how much. The price is too high, but I can't walk away, so I start to haggle. As the price begins to drop, another bowl is added, and we're back to the price we started at.

Sometime during our prolonged negotiations, a third vendor has come and is now holding on to my elbow. As I start to get the price for the two bowls down, a mantra bracelet is added, and we're back to the original price. Starting to see the futility of my predicament, I accept this price as the original vendor has a lot more bowls and bracelets that could be used to get back to that price. I advise him that I need to be let go in order to pay and all three relent. I am finally free and make my purchase.

I still have the first singing bowl and bracelet. The second bowl was donated to a Buddhist nun I knew at the time for her meditation center, which I had helped her move into. I also added a new tenet to my haggling method: No shaking hands.

Beijing Taxi Tales

China – July 2006

Being from Los Angeles, I had never ridden in a taxi before I started traveling. There are several reasons for this, including limited access, expense, and the fact that in LA everyone drives. So, I had never hopped in nor even hailed a cab until I headed out of the country. My first major international trip was to Tibet, with a few days before and after in Beijing, where my first taxi experiences occurred.

Hotel Business Card

When my tour group arrived at our Beijing hotel, our guide told us to make sure to take a business card. "Show this to any taxi driver and they will be able to return you to this hotel," he told us while distributing cards. As such, I was quite surprised when I hailed a taxi after a day of sightseeing and handed the driver the card and he seemed confused. Of course, he didn't display this confusion until after we had set off. He knew a few words of English compared to my no words of Chinese but somehow, through miming and pointing, I was able to guide him back to my hotel. I have always used landmarks instead of street names to get around, which came in handy.

Counterfeit Precautions

Our guide had also told us that there was a rash of counterfeit bills flooding the city, so to try not to use larger bills as those are the ones being faked and some vendors may not take them. I'm reminded of this a few days later when I'm taking a cab back from dinner with another couple from my tour. They agree to pay me their share in the morning and head into the hotel when we arrive. As I go to pay, I realize that I only have a large note to cover the fare. The cab driver doesn't speak English but makes it clear he won't take my money. I try to explain that it's all I have but he won't budge and I'm not sure what to do. Luckily the couple I'd traveled with came back out to see why I was delayed. They have some smaller bills and pay the now content taxi driver. Thanking them, I quickly exchange my large bill at the hotel for smaller ones to pay them back with, saying good riddance to my rejected currency.

Stop and Go (and Stop)

Beijing's traffic is hectic and slow, especially during peak times. Lines indicating lanes are just suggestions and passing on the right is always an option, even when the right is clearly not a lane. In many ways it's like LA traffic, just in slow motion. One afternoon, in peak traffic, I'm sharing a cab and sitting up front with the driver. He's growing increasingly agitated at the lack of progress and then starts veering in and out of lanes. Only we're hardly moving—so it's a rev to fill a gap I didn't think we'd be able to fill followed by a sudden slowdown. After a few times, I start to predict when he's going to do this. Even then, a few times I think "There's no way we can fit into that gap" and am surprised every time that we do. It's a talent for sure.

A Taxi That's Not a Taxi

My most interesting experience was my cab ride from the Summer Palace to a distant restaurant. July in Beijing is hot and humid, so those of us who headed out were quite ready for food and a cool down after our exploration. There are too many of us for one cab, so when we found two together near the exit, we grabbed them. Once we got going, I noticed that our "cab" does not seem to include a meter. After arriving at our restaurant, before the other cab, the driver wouldn't let us out as it's the other cab that has the meter and he doesn't know what to charge us. So, we wait in the hot car for the other driver to arrive, who seems to have taken the scenic route. Air conditioning and refreshments—so close and yet so far.

El Gringo Loco

Mexico – June 2007

I'm in Mexico to explore Barrancas del Cobre, or Copper Canyon, a group of six distinct canyons in the southwestern part of the state of Chihuahua that is four times larger than the Grand Canyon. I've joined a tour by train that's already taken us from Creel to El Fuerte and, this early morning, from El Fuerte to Barrancas, just south of Creel. We arrive at our hotel in the afternoon, which is poised on the canyon's edge near the highest point of the canyon.

From the striking view afforded from the hotel's terrace, I notice a circular structure off in the distance, which becomes the focus of a hike. I'm not exactly sure how to get there but a brief exploration behind the hotel finds what turns out to be the beginning of a trail. As I start to head out, I realize that I am alone and have told no one where I am going. I am also traversing along the edge of the canyon at an elevation of around 8000 feet and left my hiking boots at home, so I'm attempting it with sneakers.

The hike is going well until I come across a short ladder made of weathered wood missing its bottom rung that is the only way up a tall boulder. I have long legs, so it's not a problem overcoming the missing step. I continue on along the boulders and narrow path until I now encounter a broken bridge, the first few feet of which are missing. This poses more of a dilemma. Should I turn around? Should I try to find another way across? Never being one to let obstacles get in my way, I decided to jump and continue on.

My goal now in sight, I come across my final obstacle: a narrow wooden pole with notches cut into it acting as a ladder up to the structure

I'm aiming to reach. It again comes to mind that I am alone and have told no one where I have gone and am only one slip from a very long fall. But I've come too far to stop now. I slowly ascend like a tightrope walker to the circular structure, though still have no idea what it is. It does offer some stunning views of the canyon, so I get in some photos.

It starts to gently rain, so I quickly return back to the hotel following a different route that doesn't cling to the side of the canyon, though does take me through someone's property at one point. Rain now subsided; I head back to the terrace for a drink only to find that several of my group had been following my hike with the binoculars they'd brought for birding. "We really didn't think you'd jump," they tell me as I'm offered a few drinks. I like to think the locals tell stories of "el gringo loco" who overcame three obstacles to reach his destination, though the hotel staff probably just warn others not to attempt what this crazy gringo did.

My Man in Cusco

Peru – December 2007

Christmas and I have an unconventional relationship. When I was very young, my parents and I did have a traditional Christmas tree complete with ornaments, lights, and garland and the requisite wrapped presents underneath. Over time, however, the tree was replaced with a stuffed penguin wearing antlers in a sleigh and the presents were put inside a large trashcan so our dogs wouldn't destroy them. An added benefit of the trashcan was that, after all the presents were unwrapped and opened, the wrapping paper and boxes could go back into it for easy cleanup.

As such, I prefer to be away during the holidays. For this Christmas, I've chosen to be in Peru and, on Christmas day, Cusco. I should point out that Christmas Eve in Peru, at least in Cusco, is like New Year's Eve in the States, with lots of music, dancing, and alcohol. I didn't realize this when booking the trip but ended up going out with a few in my group for dancing and drinks and ended up not returning until after 4 a.m., much to the chagrin of my roommate. This was also the night I learned I have a high tolerance for vodka (my Russian ancestors would be proud).

While the others I'd been out with are sleeping it off, I'm out and about early to enjoy Cusco on Christmas day, which is full of people and pageants. We've been in town a few days and I have become used to every vendor approaching me to sell something, but I was not prepared for Jimmy. Unlike other sellers who have a stall to display their wares, Jimmy is on foot with just two paintings he's offering to sell. They are painted by him, he says, though they look exactly like all the other paintings being sold throughout the city.

I politely tell Jimmy that I'm not interested, but he continues to tell me that profits from his sales go to support his school supplies. Jimmy seems to be around sixteen and, being mobile, isn't going to take no for an answer lightly. I again let him know I'm not interested, so he changes tactic, or at least product. Would I be interested in some knives? He can take me to a nearby shop with some lovely examples. I do love a good knife, but can't imagine getting one through Customs and besides, I thought Jimmy was an artist.

Clearly not deterred by my lack of interest in paintings or knives, Jimmy now offers some beautiful women only a few blocks from the Cathedral. Now I'm not Catholic but offering up a prostitute only a few blocks from a Cathedral on Christmas seems like some kind of sin and now I'm a sinner-by-association. I let Jimmy provide a few more details as we are heading toward the aforementioned Cathedral, which I duck into in an attempt to lose Jimmy, figuring pimps probably don't attend Christmas mass. I typically don't either but wait twenty minutes inside, hoping he's found another mark during this time.

Jimmy isn't there when I re-emerge from the church, but I know he's out there somewhere. If you ever have a need for paintings, knives, or beautiful women, he's your man in Cusco.

A Disappointing Drawbridge

Peru – December 2007

Once you're done exploring the ruins of Machu Picchu, you have several options. The most popular is to climb Huayna Picchu, the dome shaped mountain behind the ruins in the classic Machu Picchu photo, but it's not an easy climb and requires a permit, which sells out quickly. Alternatively, you can climb Machu Picchu Mountain, which doesn't require a permit and offers the classic view with Huayna Picchu in the background. You could also hike to the Sun Gate, which is how those who hiked the Inca Trail enter the site. Or, you can do what I did, and head to the Inca Drawbridge.

Someone coming from that direction tells me it is only five to ten minutes to reach it. After twenty minutes of walking a slippery path along the edge of a steep canyon wall, I consult my Lonely Planet guide to find that it is "under a half-hour's walk." Another five or so minutes and I finally reach the bridge. It's a narrow opening into the location and it's a rather busy viewpoint, so I have to wait for a few people to exit before entering.

Lonely Planet also notes that "you'll have to be content with photographing the bridge from a distance, as someone crossed the bridge some years ago and tragically fell to their death." What they leave out is that, after walking thirty minutes, it's a disappointing payoff. Essentially, it's a gap in a narrow path covered by some planks of wood. I know the Inca's were incredible engineers, but I have a sneaking suspicion that's not the original wood. I'm also not sure where the "draw" in the drawbridge title comes from, as those planks seem rather stationary.

So that I haven't walked all this way for nothing, I snap a few photos and then ask one of the others there if they can take my photo with the bridge in the background. I want to both prove I made the effort and provide a sense of scale for this underwhelming site.

Araceli's Flower

Honduras – July 2008

It's looking for a while like we might not make it to Honduras. We're in Santiago Atitlán, Guatemala, and today is meant to be a travel day to Copán Ruinas, Honduras. We set out in the morning but after an hour have to turn back due to the road being blocked by a mudslide caused by heavy rains in the night. Back to Atitlán and then onto a second route but, after less than an hour this time, we discover this direction has also been blocked by a mudslide. This leaves only a lesser used southern route known for bandits that like to hold up tour buses. Our guide seems a little anxious about taking this route and lines up an armored guard to follow our bus to the border.

When we finally arrive at the border, it's a simple crossing but then we find that the main bridge into Copán has been washed out. I'm starting to get the feeling someone doesn't want us to arrive. And the rain begins anew. It's dark and wet when we arrive, but we do arrive and the next day is spent exploring the wonderful ruins of Copán (not to be mistaken for Copán Ruinas, the name of the town beside the ruins of Copán.)

The following day a group of us had wanted to go zip-lining but have been advised that it's not safe due to all of the rain. Instead, our guide arranges for horseback riding to the small village of Los Sapos. A van picks us up at our hotel and takes us to where the horses are waiting. The handler takes one look at me, a head higher than everyone else, and leaves to return with a horse a few hands taller than the others. We mount up and head for the village.

I notice that my horse starts out in the lead, then slowly lets every other horse move past him only to then speed up and get back into the lead once he's realized he's last. He repeats this pattern until we arrive at the village, which makes conversing with fellow riders a little challenging. Once we arrive, we are set upon by a collection of young girls selling flowers made out of corn husks. There's a bit of a walk from where we have dismounted up to the village and there seems to be one girl for each of us. The smallest of the group, Araceli, has decided to stick to my side with her flower.

She is barefoot and the path is both muddy and rutted and it's not long before she's tripped and hurt herself. She starts to cry, which puts me into a bit of a guilt trip. I don't want a corn husk flower and I don't have any local currency on me, but it seems I should buy the flower she's still holding as I'm the reason she's tripped. The one girl who speaks English has come over to help her and I tell her that I only have U.S. dollars. She says that's okay, so I hand a dollar to Araceli, who has recovered from her tumble. She is hesitant at first because it's not Honduran lempira, but the girl who speaks English tells her in Spanish that it's okay, so she hands me her flower and now she's happy.

Whether a con or an accident, I rode back down from the village with Araceli's flower securely tucked in my shirt pocket and carefully packed it for the remainder of the trip. It sits today on a shelf among many other souvenirs, irreplaceable and treasured.

Into the Yukon with Mopps

Canada – July 2008

Many years ago, I felt a call to Alaska. Unfortunately, lack of money and time left it just a calling. A few years later I contemplated applying for a teaching position there as it would give me an excuse to go north for the interview. I didn't apply, so when I was given the opportunity to go on an Alaskan glacier cruise a little later, I jumped at it. While I'd never considered a cruise before, I figured I'd get to sign up for some semi-adventurous shore excursions. Semi-adventurous as I've only just recovered from an ankle injury that saw me using a cane for six-months and I don't want to push my luck.

I grew up watching reruns of Rocky and Bullwinkle on TV, so I can't think of Skagway without thinking of Dudley Do-Right, who along with his faithful dog, Faithful Dog, defeated archvillain Snidely Whiplash in a dogsledding contest there. I'm not in Skagway for a dogsledding contest, however, but rather as the entry point for doing some off-roading in Canada's Yukon Territory in four-wheel drive Jeeps.

Each Jeep holds four passengers and the plan is that at each stop we switch drivers, but I'm teamed with a family of three from the U.K. that doesn't have insurance, so all the driving is on me. Seems my luck is running good for this outing as I was really hoping to be behind the wheel for the four-wheel driving. We leave Skagway, passing through such uplifting areas as Dead Horse Gulch and Tormented Valley, making our first stop at Fraser, just after clearing Canadian Customs. Next it's Tutshi Lake, just a little more north. Then we're into Carcross and officially in the Yukon.

We've been in a small convoy of about six vehicles with our guide, Mopps, in the lead Jeep conveying information to us between stops through a radio system. Just before the off-roading begins, we stop at a convenience store that offers a do-it-yourself passport stamp, which some of us indulge in. It's an unofficial stamp but so is the one I received at Machu Picchu (and many more I will collect in the future). We then get ready to start our off-roading. The last time I was in a Jeep with four-wheel drive engaged was when I used to live in the mountains and bought a Jeep for the commute up and down.

The off-roading portion of the outing isn't going off-road to see a site, but rather a rough area beside the store that is more like a test track. Not exactly what I was expecting, but it's fun nonetheless. As I'm not alone, I do take it a little slower than I usually would. After about thirty minutes of ups and downs and side to sides, we start the drive back to Skagway.

Once back in Skagway, I decide to walk into town for lunch. Mopps recommends a place and tells me to look up a pretty bartender there with a tattoo on her arm named Kat, so I do.

Birthday Impromptu

Costa Rica – August 2008

I've been given the chance to visit Costa Rica as part of a visiting party from my college. One of our counselors is trying to resurrect a study abroad program and I'd mentioned an idea I had that could expand the usual offering, so I was added to the team. Along with visiting the center she's hoping to start up the program with, we'll also be visiting a local high school, where I'll pitch an idea of having visiting professors tutoring students in need before college entrance exams, which will lead to a photo of me and the principal shaking hands in his office.

We'll each be doing a home stay, with visits to work related sites during the day and free time in the late afternoons and evenings. I'm placed with a family with a young son around eight years old. They don't speak any English and my Spanish is poor, but we make do. By the end of my time with them, I'm helping the mother study geometry for an exam at the dining room table with the use of a Spanish-English dictionary. When their son comes home from school each day, we head to his bedroom to play video games. I've never played any of the games before, but between hand gestures and observation, I catch on.

One night I notice there's a cake and a two-liter bottle of cola set out on the dining room table. Something is up as this is the first time I've seen soda in the house. I soon realize that it's the son's birthday and I feel awful for not knowing. The family has let me stay with them and the mother had been doing my laundry and making up my room, and I have nothing to give their son on his birthday. Think, dammit.

My father was an artist and for over a decade hosted a public broadcasting television show on cartooning. His belief was that anyone can draw, and he had a trick to get anyone started using the word "go," which forms the eyes and nose of a face. I used to draw when I was younger but didn't want to compete with him, which is one reason I took to photography when I discovered it.

I now think of his "go" trick and grab a piece of paper. If I add the son's spikey hair and a few other features, I'll have a cartoon of him. My impromptu gift is looking good, so I add "¡Feliz Cumpleaños!" and his name to my sketch and hold the drawing up next to him to try to indicate that it's meant to be of him and is my gift. The parents catch my drift and the son seems to appreciate it, especially the spikey hair.

Thank you, dad.

Trying to Avoid a Stoning in Fez

Morocco – June 2009

The medina in Fez is filled with compact, windy streets, indescribable scents, and cries of "Balak! Balak!" when an unyielding donkey is approaching. It reminds me of the Amazon in that it is nearly impossible to be put into words—it really needs to be experienced. From tanneries to rug shops, you can find it here. Delve deep enough and one can probably still find a Minotaur.

It's probably not surprising then to discover that Fez is a rather traditional town. I'm travelling with a group with only four solo travelers—myself, a Kiwi accompanying a couple from New Zealand, a well-travelled but very peculiar Brit, and a leggy blonde from Nebraska. We started in Spain, worked our way down Portugal, and are now in Morocco. The leggy blonde and I have started wandering about together (and avoiding the peculiar Brit).

The afternoon we arrive in Fez I decide to head out to exchange some money and buy a few provisions before dinner. At dinner the leggy blonde asks if I wouldn't mind taking her to the same exchange and market that evening. One problem: She decides to wear rather short shorts and a strappy top for the outing. I start to notice the damning looks almost immediately once we are on the main street, especially from the local women.

At the exchange, the man behind the counter won't look her way, so I complete the transaction on her behalf. More damning stares on our way to the market. Again, the seller won't even look at her, so I use my limited French to make the purchase. As we head back to the hotel,

I note that she might want to cover up a bit while we're in Morocco as I have a feeling that, if not, she's going to end up being stoned and I'm going to be arrested for being in the company of a salacious woman.

The next morning, she comes down with legs covered and a top with sleeves. She lets me know that her fiancé appreciated my accompanying her to the exchange and market, and for the recommendation to cover up. He was worried she wouldn't and might find herself in some trouble. He'd also be appreciative when, a few days later, I am offered twenty camels for her but respectfully decline.

The Wandering Wallet

Czech Republic – July 2009

Apparently, I have a trustworthy face. On more than one occasion, people I have been traveling with, who had never met me before, have had me collect their money for tips for guides and drivers. Guides have even asked me to help collect passports or post their tour packets back to their companies for them. One even handed me his wallet before each overnight train as he was a sound sleeper and figured it was safer with me. So, this is how I ended up stealing another guide's wallet.

I'm in the Czech Republic as part of a Central Europe tour that started in Austria. It's advertised as an Eastern European tour, but our guide is adamant that it is a Central European tour. He's young, Slovakian, and likes to end each day with drinks. As my roommate is Australian, he joins him every night. I decide to also join them this night, along with two others from our group. As the drinks progress, we notice that the guide leaves his wallet on the table and seems to become less and less aware of it as the night progresses.

"Someone should take it," one of my group states as the guide is off getting more drinks. We each look at each other before it's decided that it should be me as he would never expect it would be me. So I do, slipping it into the side pocket of my cargo pants. And, as tends to happen when many drinks are involved, he doesn't notice when we got up to leave and I am only reminded when I return to my room and notice a bulge in one of pants pockets. Unless there's a knock at the door, I guess I'll be returning it in the morning.

There was no knock, so I bring the wallet with me to breakfast. Our guide has either been told it was me or has figured it out, as he comes up to me as soon as he sees me. I should mention that I have a good head for numbers. I have all my vital numbers—passport, driver's license, credit cards—memorized and can tell you my hotel room numbers for every room of a trip. I can also tell you my grandparent's phone number from when I was a kid, though both they and the house are long gone. It's a gift and a curse.

So, when I hand our guide his wallet, I tell him it's okay, I've already memorized his credit card number. I then start to recite the first few digits, just enough to see a troubled look appear on his face. I imagine him checking his next credit card statement carefully and don't notice him leaving his wallet on the table anymore.

Silver and Bones

Czech Republic – July 2009

Kutna Hora is about an hour's train ride from Prague, with trains leaving the main train station every few hours. In the 14th century, Kutna Hora rivaled Prague as Bohemia's most important town. This was due to the silver ore that ran through the rocks beneath it. Then, as tends to happen, the silver ran out.

The town began in 1142 with the settlement of Sedlec Abbey, the first Cistercian monastery in Bohemia. By 1260, German miners began to mine for silver in the mountain region, which was part of the monastery property. The town is also home to St. Barbara's Church, whose construction was begun in 1388 but, due to many interruptions, not completed until 1905. Gothic in design, it was originally intended to be probably twice its current size. It is a striking site, but not the reason I am here.

Kutna Hora is probably most known today for the Sedlec Ossuary, a small Roman Catholic chapel, located beneath the Cemetery Church of All Saints. The ossuary contains approximately 40,000 to 70,000 human skeletons that have been artistically arranged to form decorations and furnishings for the chapel. Four immense bell-shaped mounds occupy the corners of the chapel, while an enormous chandelier of bones, which contains at least one of every bone in the human body, hangs from the center of the nave with garlands of skulls draping the vault. It is not for the faint of heart.

As the area was founded on silver, it makes sense to end my day trip with a mining tour. Before entering the mine, we're given a white cloth coat (offering visibility, not protection), a hard hat, and a war surplus light that cannot be moved more than 90 degrees in any direction without having battery acid spill out. At first the cave we have entered is rather spacious, but we're warned that the shaft gets low and narrow at points, very narrow.

When we're before the narrowest and shortest point, I volunteer to go first. I figure, given my height and girth, if I can make it through, then so can anyone in my group. If not, then I have a whole group of people behind me who can push. Always good to forward plan.

Lost in Transit: Arriving

Tunisia – December 2009

I was not supposed to be here. I'd planned out a month-long trip through Southeast Asia that perfectly filled my winter break. However, it meant that I had to depart no later than Saturday, December 12. Slight problem: One of my best friends was getting married on Sunday, December 13. Back to the drawing board.

While I had considered other trips besides Southeast Asia, looking over them now that I needed an alternative, I came to the realization that none really interested me anymore. Then I received a catalog from a tour company I had traveled with before and noticed they had started offering a week-long trip to Tunisia and that got my attention. Traveling from Southern California to Tunisia for less than ten days wasn't the best plan, but Tunisia was a country I'd always wanted to visit, and something was better than nothing.

Normally I fly through Los Angeles, which is a ninety-minute drive from my house in good traffic. As flying to Tunis was going to require a layover anyway, I decide instead to fly from Ontario, which is less than a thirty-minute drive. It's not an ideal route—Ontario to Salt Lake City to Paris to Tunis—but it beats having to deal with LA traffic.

While waiting for my delayed Salt Lake City flight, I receive a text from Air France letting me know my Tunis flight had been cancelled and thanking me for my understanding. After nearly an hour on hold, I reach someone at Air France who confirms that my Tunis flight has been cancelled but they can get me on the last flight out that day. Just as this is being completed, they realize that since I originally booked with a different carrier, I'd have to contact that carrier to complete the transaction. When I do, they do not show that my Tunis flight has been cancelled, so I head to Paris with the status of my Tunis flight unknown.

As my connection to Paris is now under fifteen minutes, I'm moved to the very front of the plane so that I have the best chance of making the flight. Once in Salt Lake City, I'm let off first and make a mad dash for my Paris connection. I just make it, then sit on the tarmac for over an hour because the plane is overweight, and they need passengers to volunteer to disembark and stay the night.

I arrive in Paris nearly two hours late and head to a long line for Air France filled with other passengers who have missed their connections. When it's finally my turn, I am informed that yes, my flight was cancelled (though I would have missed it anyway) but they can get me on a flight leaving the next day, getting me to Tunis by 3 p.m. As the tour I am joining is leaving that morning, I suggest just returning me to California. Suddenly, a place for me is found on the 9 p.m. flight, which doesn't depart until 11 p.m., landing in Tunis just before 1 a.m.

By 2 a.m. it's clear that my luggage did not make it, so it's off to another long line at lost luggage. I had fully intended on traveling with only carry-ons this trip but changed my mind at the last minute. Now I'm stuck with a day pack that essentially carries only my camera, travel guide, and phone. To make matters worse, every so often a load of found luggage is brought out and you have to make the choice of staying in line and assuming your bag is not there or getting out of line to see if you're lucky. I wasn't lucky.

A lost luggage claim finally filed (thank you high school French), I arrive at my hotel at 4:30 a.m. to discover I have a 6:30 a.m. wake-up call scheduled. I shower and clean my clothes as best I can. I try to rest a bit but am awoken at 6 a.m. by the day's first call to prayer from a nearby minaret. When I finally meet my guide, she informs me that I'll be able to retrieve my lost luggage only when we return to Tunis, which is in five days. Time to improvise.

I don't join my tour for breakfast, opting instead to try to get a bit more rest in my room, so the first time I see any of them is on the bus. That's when I notice a striking Chinese woman who appears to be traveling with her mother. My journal from that time notes "a beautiful Chinese woman with a lovely British accent" and further, inaccurately records that "I could be smitten if there wasn't the fact that we'll never see each other again." She'd later become my wife.

Lost in Transit: Departing

Tunisia – December 2009

My first evening in Tunisia finds us in Sfax, Tunisia's second largest city. Nearby our hotel is a market where I'm able to pick up some toiletries, underthings, and a few shirts. So now I'm living out of a day pack and two plastic bags. We return to Tunis on Christmas day and I make a run to the airport to retrieve my lost bag. I'm told there is a large room full of unclaimed bags I will get to sort through. I have visions of the end of *Raiders of the Lost Ark*, when the Ark of the Covenant is being placed into storage. The reality is not quite so expansive. The bags are sorted by airline, though mine is not among the lost bags for Air France. Out of the corner of my eye I catch the back of my bag and we are finally reunited.

I am joined by someone else from our tour who had also lost her luggage, but her bag is nowhere to be found. I'm anxious to return to our hotel as I have a beautiful Chinese woman waiting, who is probably wondering why I'm not joining her for dinner as by then I was sharing all of my meals with her, but it's Christmas and the only airline official to be found doesn't speak English. My high school French is strained, though we do eventually learn that her bag has not been found and she's given instructions on how to file a claim for the loss.

The day of my returning flights starts off well. That evening I say goodbye to my future wife and we exchange contact information. My flight from Tunis to Paris departs and arrives on time. I make it through security in Paris and find my gate. Due to a failed al-Qa'ida bombing attempt two days prior, where a passenger tried to set off chemical explosives sewn to his underwear on a flight from Amsterdam to Detroit, there is extra security at the gate. Shoes and jackets are removed, passengers are frisked front and back, and large carry-ons are checked and smaller carry-ons are thoroughly searched. Subsequently, we arrive in Atlanta late and I find I've just missed my connecting flight. So, it's another day living out of my day pack. I contact the airline to see if they can put me up for the night but as the delay was not their fault, they can only offer me a new flight the following day. As for an accommodation, I'm on my own. I head for the hotel shuttles and find one to what I know is a reasonably priced hotel. Fortunately, the receptionist takes pity on me and puts together a toiletry assortment.

In the morning I'm expecting a direct flight from Atlanta to Ontario but instead find I am flying to Denver, then Salt Lake City, and finally Ontario. In Denver I get shaky and realize all I've had to eat the prior twelve hours was orange juice for dinner and a large coffee for breakfast, so I find myself a cafe and resist the temptation to order a Denver omelet. The remaining flights are uneventful.

When I finally do make it to Ontario, my bag is not among those on the baggage carousel. When I head to lost luggage, I see it sitting in the back of the room—it had made the connecting flight from Atlanta without me. In all I've lost nearly two days during this trip due to cancelations and delays, which I intend to make up in bed. I do send out a quick email before retiring, letting my future wife know why I had seemingly disappeared for two days.

A Disputed Territory (and Guidebook)

Azerbaijan – June 2010

You learn a few things while traveling. One is that some of the fiercest enemies tend to be neighbors. When I was in Armenia, two of its four borders with neighboring countries were closed. Its border with Turkey was closed due to that country's denial of the atrocities committed against Armenia nearly a century before, and its border with Azerbaijan was closed due to a disputed territory in Armenia that was gifted to Azerbaijan by Stalin in the 1920s.

Something else traveling teaches you is to be weary of quiet border crossings. The officials there tend to be bored and have nothing but time on their hands. I'm crossing into Azerbaijan through Georgia in part because its border with Armenia is closed. In fact, the night before, our guide tells my group that anything mentioning Armenia or written in Armenian may be confiscated at the border. As Armenia was the first Christian country, my souvenir is a New Testament written in Armenian, which I made sure to well conceal as I don't want it taken.

Unfortunately, it's a quiet border between Georgia and Azerbaijan. You exit Georgia then walk about a kilometer of no man's land to the checkpoint in Azerbaijan. As we're the only ones crossing, the Azerbaijani officials decide to look through the luggage of every other person with a fine-toothed comb. I should have been the first chosen as I was initially second in line, but one in our group cut in front of me just as our line was forming, so she got her luggage well inspected while I was able to smuggle my Armenian New Testament across without incident.

Many of us are carrying the same Lonely Planet guidebook that covers the three countries of our tour—Armenia, Georgia, and

Azerbaijan—but only one of us had taken extensive notes in their copy and he was one of the ones inspected and his guidebook confiscated. The officials didn't like that the book included information on both Armenia and Azerbaijan, due to the conflicted territory. Thinking it may be because they thought the book lists the territory as Armenian, our guide shows the officials that it includes Nagorno-Karabakh in a separate chapter, but they still won't have it.

After my unfortunate companion made it through, I offer him my copy of the guidebook, but he declines his notes are lost and we only have a few days left to travel. I then notice an old-timer from our group, who also made it through unscathed, take out his camera. Not wanting to draw attention to him, I tell him under my breath that he should put it away. By now we're nearly all across and I don't want this being the reason those of us who weren't searched are now searched. He puts his camera away but a few minutes later I catch him at it again. Small talk has never been my strong point, but I come up with something to discuss to distract him until we're all safely across, less one Lonely Planet guide.

Form over Function

Bosnia and Herzegovina – June 2010

My wife and I are taking a local bus from Dubrovnik, Croatia, to Sarajevo. As it's a local bus, there is no English spoken, meaning when we stop, we don't know if it's a short break to stretch our legs or a longer stop for lunch. The result being that when we do arrive in Sarajevo six hours later, we're starving.

We head to our hotel and ask the receptionist where there's a good place to eat. She recommends a restaurant around the corner, so we quickly drop off our bags in our room and head for an early dinner. The waiter is a little taken aback when we order three meals, but he brings them, and they are quickly consumed. We wander a bit about the old town before settling in for the night.

When we return to our hotel, the receptionist asks how we liked her choice and also mentions that some guests have had difficulty operating the shower, so if that turns out to be the case, just give her a call. "How hard can it be to operate a shower?" I think as we head back to our room.

As we were in a hunger-induced haze when we dropped off our bags, we hadn't really noticed how modern our room is. I'd selected the hotel based on price and location and am surprised how contemporary it is, considering we're just off the old town. Speaking of which, let's figure out this shower.

Below the shower head is what appears to be a shiny silver brick. I'm figuring there should be a way to turn either end, with one side starting the water and the other adjusting the temperature. A careful inspection reveals it's solid, like the monolith in *2001: A Space Odyssey*. Okay, maybe you pull it out from the wall. No, it doesn't seem to budge. Okay, maybe it rotates—still no luck. Now I know why the receptionist said to give her a call.

It's another ten minutes of trying to figure out this puzzle box of a shower when I give in and give the receptionist a call. The solution has to do with applying a certain amount of pressure while simultaneously rotating and pulling at a specific angle. Who designed this thing? I follow her directions and we soon have a functioning shower. I tell my wife I'm not convinced I'll be able to get it operating a second time, so she should shower after me.

Then I notice the toilet, which is encased in a semi-opaque and rather thick glass. Another interesting design choice. Not only is the door to the toilet rather heavy (I'm beginning to believe it is bullet-proof, which would explain its thickness), it also makes a loud snap when opening or closing it. So, if you're looking for some privacy in the middle of the night, be prepared to wake someone up. And, if you're looking for a prime example of form over function in design, I've found the place for you.

Camel-Jacked

Egypt – December 2010

I have wanted to visit Egypt since elementary school, when my fifth-grade class made a school presentation and I was in charge of narrating the section on ancient Egypt. I quickly became enamored with pyramids and hieroglyphics. It was also around this time that the King Tut exhibit came to Los Angeles, seeing my mom and I standing in a long line, eager to witness history. It is also a country visited by the father of history, Herodotus. He writes in Chapter 2 of *The Histories*, "Concerning Egypt itself I shall extend my remarks to a great length, because there is no country that possesses so many wonders, nor any that has such a number of works which defy description."

We arrive in Cairo an hour late, only we're staying in Giza, not Cairo, so it's another hour to our hotel. The following day is a full one, beginning with the pyramids at Giza. The Great Pyramid is the Pyramid of Khufu (or Cheops in Greek). While this is the largest of the pyramids here, I spend most of my time exploring the Pyramid of Khafre. This pyramid is distinct as its top still has some of the limestone casing that once covered the entire pyramid.

While on my way to explore the Great Pyramid, I am pulled beside a camel and a cloth is tied around my head. "Good photo," I'm told by the camel handler. Next thing I know, I'm atop the camel and am being paraded around for more "good photos." Just when I think I'm finally being let down, the owner jumps in front of my camel and leads us to a secluded spot to ask for money. I tell him that I have no money, my wife has our money. As we continue this back-and-forth, my wife catches up with me and I ask her to pay for my rescue.

Surprisingly, this is not the only time I'm unintentionally on a camel this trip. About a week later, we're on a boat taking us to a Nubian village for the night. When we come ashore, I'm the first off, only to discover that this stop is solely for those who wanted to ride a camel into the village—nearly everyone else is still on the boat, including my confused wife. I'm already off the boat, so might as well go by camel the rest of the way. All goes smoothly until I notice that the rest of my group is going up a hill whereas I'm going down a different path. Turns out it's a shortcut to the finish point and my camel handler wants to ask for more money before the others arrive.

When we return to Luxor, tensions are high as a Coptic Christian church was attacked only a few days before in Alexandria. A few weeks later the January 25 Revolution begins, and we witness sites we'd just been to being vandalized or destroyed. Unfortunately, this will not be the first or last time such an occurrence has happened after our travels.

Night Train to Luxor

Egypt – December 2010

My wife and I have been on many sleeper trains over the years. The best by far was our overnight train from Cairo to Luxor. We had a private room—just two beds, a sink, and even a small closet. The porter who setup our room for the night and brought our dinner would also bring us a light breakfast in the morning. So far so good.

All was going well until I needed to use the restroom. We'd just completed our dinner, so I thought I'd dash to the facilities before everyone else had the same idea. Our compartment is in the front of our railcar and the restroom is at the end. As I am washing my hands, the lights go out. I give my eyes a moment to adjust, then slide the door open. I pause for a second as I notice the lights are out in the entire car when the train hits a bump and the door slams shut. Problem: my thumb is between the door and its destination.

I slowly make my way back to our room in the darkness and in pain. At least being in the front compartment means I won't mistakenly pop into someone else's room. I use the small flashlight I always travel with to find pain pills. There's only a small amount of blood, though the thumb is pounding. I clean it up in the sink. As the room is dark, the only thing to do is go to sleep, so we turn in for the night.

Just as the pounding begins to subside and I start to drift off to sleep, the train comes to its first curve, which it seems to be taking a bit too fast as screeching brakes can be heard that jerk the cabin about a bit. It's noisy but quick. A few minutes later, it happens again. So, I'm back up with the flashlight to find my earplugs. Relief from the screeching, but not the jerking around every curve and there are a lot of curves.

I'm reminded of the drivers back home who speed between stop signs. Even when they can see the next stop sign from the one they're currently stopped at, they accelerate and then slam on their brakes. The big difference being that they have seatbelts and would only experience some forward momentum when hitting their brakes, whereas we have nothing holding us in place and our momentum is side to side.

Being tall, I never quite fit on sleeper train beds, but I use this to my advantage by extending my legs a bit to the wall at the end of the bed to form a brace for myself. Not the most comfortable position, but it provides some stability and I don't think I'm going to get much sleep anyway if the route is this unsteady all the way. At least it's a nice room.

Ashes to Ashes

Israel – June 2011

The year I turn forty is also the year my mom turns sixty and I thought a good way to celebrate would be to take her to Israel. Unfortunately, a few years before this she was diagnosed with bladder cancer and she lost her battle with it just a month before turning sixty. She let me know that she wanted to be cremated but made me promise not to keep her ashes "in a damn urn." I knew what I needed to do.

My wife has an aunt who resides in Israel with her Israeli husband, so we asked if we could visit during my summer break. I wasn't entirely sure where I would spread my mother's ashes or even if I could get them through Israel's intense security, I just knew I had a promise to keep.

I've only ever been called into the little room beside the immigration windows on two occasions, once in Dubai and this time in Tel Aviv. As we are visiting my wife's family, we decided it would be best to let her do the talking. For some reason, the immigration official doesn't seem to understand how my wife, who is Chinese, could have an aunt, also Chinese, living and working in Israel. She explains that she lives in Israel with her Israeli husband. "Is she an Israeli citizen?" she is asked. When replying yes, the response is, "How can that be?"

After a few more minutes of this back-and-forth, a second immigration official arrives, seems just as confused, and we're asked to follow her to a sitting area while our passports are taken away. A few more minutes pass before I'm called into the little room, which consists of a desk and another official. I'm asked to have a seat and then I'm ignored while the official types on his computer and then gets up to consult with a colleague. I can see our passports sitting on the desk between us, so that's something.

Thinking of the confusion being caused earlier, I use this time to develop a strategy. When my existence is finally acknowledged and I start being asked the same questions that seemed to confuse the officials outside, I go into teacher mode. I say that I am an American, pointing to my U.S. passport, traveling with my wife, pointing to her U.K. passport. The passports are open to their respective photo pages, so I point to my wife's photo and note that my wife is Chinese and we are here to visit her aunt, also Chinese (pointing again to the passport picture) whose is married to an Israeli. I am speaking slowly and calmly and hoping the visual aids help. They do, as the new official seems to approve of my explaining and soon our passports are stamped and back in my possession.

Finally in the country, I decide to spread my mother's ashes in the Sea of Galilee, finding a quiet spot for my final moment with her. Before leaving the country, I tell my wife that I think I should do the talking on the way out and simply tell them that we were in the country to visit my Israeli uncle. Given my full name, Jeremiah Abraham, it seems to me a much easier story for them to follow, and it doesn't hurt that it's also true.

Two for Ten Thouuuuuusaaaaaand!

Indonesia – June 2011

Besakih Temple, often referred to as Bali's "Mother Temple," sits high on the southwestern slopes of Mount Agung. It is considered to be the largest and holiest of the island's temples and, to the Balinese, visiting the temple sanctuaries of Besakih is a special pilgrimage. Many stairs lead up to the sacred mountainside, leading to the many temples that vary according to type, status, and function.

Pura Besakih features three main temples dedicated to the Hindu trinity. Pura Penataran Agung has white banners for Shiva, the destroyer; Pura Kiduling Kreteg features red banners for Brahma, the creator; and Pura Batu Madeg represents Vishnu, the preserver, with its black banners. One can visit many other smaller temples in the complex, but often their inner courtyards are closed to the public as they're reserved for pilgrims. Pura Besakih is the only temple open to every devotee from any caste. This is due to its role as the primal center of all ceremonial activities.

While a beautiful and expansive location, one is followed the whole time by young girls selling packs of postcards. Outside the temple complex, from the parking area to the stairs, one hears the incessant cry of "One for 10,000!" At the time, 10,000 Indonesian rupiah is a little over $1. Inside the complex the offer becomes "Two for 10,000!" This offer follows you everywhere—outside temples, inside temples, resting at the top—from every direction and from dozens of girls and is pronounced "Two for ten thouuuuuusaaaaaand!"

My wife finally gives in while heading out of the complex, figuring this will silence the offers. No such luck. We continue to be followed and offered packets of postcards. Even when one of the girls is informed that postcards have already been purchased, she simply replies, "But not from me!"

Paris Metro Pros and Cons

France – July 2011

Saturday, July 2

I have to say that I like the Paris metro system. Unlike its London counterpart, it is more spacious, better ventilated, and less hectic. The performers often found in London tube stations actually board the trains in Paris, offering a song for a stop or two. London trains always seem too cramped for this to ever happen.

That said, it does lull one into a false sense of security. This is a foreign city with every tourist a potential target for pickpockets—some young, knowing they will only get a hand slap if caught, and others earning their living this way. I will blame it on being road weary for inexplicably putting all of my travel documents and money into my travel wallet this morning (something I would normally never do). Whether young or old, I made someone's day today.

It is an odd sensation realizing that you have no money and no identification. It is also an odd sensation calling credit card companies from Paris while waiting to be called into a police station to file a report, which is needed by the consulate to get a temporary passport. And here I thought turning forty would be uninteresting.

Sunday, July 3

I wake up in the middle of the night with a horrid realization: While Paris does not celebrate the July 4th holiday, the American consulate does. As it's the weekend, this means the soonest I can go in is on Tuesday the 5th, not Monday the 4th, which is also the day of our train ride back to London. Of course, this is assuming I can even get into the consulate without any form of ID. I eventually fall back asleep only to wake again with another realization: If I can login to my work email and get access to a printer, I had to send a scan of my driver's license to Human Resources a few months back for some forgotten reason. Thank you, academic bureaucracy.

We spend the first part of my birthday retracing our steps along the metro system from where I last saw my wallet to when I discovered it missing and asking if anyone had turned one into lost and found. We both knew this wouldn't be the case, but it felt like something should be done. And it kept my mind from focusing on the various Draconian ways I was imagining pickpockets should be punished should such punishment be left up to me.

Monday, July 4

In the morning we head to a photo studio were I can get some passport photos taken and make a dry run out to the consulate. I had called the consulate on Saturday after my passport was stolen and was surprised that I was unable to report it stolen as I was not able to speak to someone. I understand that I cannot get it replaced until they opened again the following week, but would have at least thought they'd like to know the number of a passport that had been lifted. Instead, I was sent to their website to download paperwork that I wasn't sure at the time I'd be able to print.

Tuesday, July 5

It's an early rise to arrive at the consulate by 7:45 a.m. to be first in line. Fortunately, our hotel had allowed me use of their computer and printer, so I was able to print my scanned driver's license and consulate paperwork. I'm called from the waiting area to my first window around

9:00 a.m., where I turn in the paperwork I had downloaded along with my police report and am asked to explain my situation. I'm sent back to the waiting area before being called to another window where a more official looking official has me go over my story again in greater detail. He seems satisfied and sends me to another window to pay the fee and submit my passport photos. Then back to the waiting area.

Many more people have arrived by now and I begin hearing similar stories to my own being told. I can't hear everything being said but can make out "metro" and "pickpocket" spoken repeatedly. By 10:15 a.m. I'm called to my last window of the morning and am handed my temporary passport. I'm told by the last official that had I arrived an hour later, I probably would not have gotten my passport in time to catch my train.

So it's back to the hotel to gather our bags, then off to the train station to board our afternoon train. It's an uneventful return to London, though the immigration official in London does give my temporary passport an odd look as one usually only uses one to enter their home country. "Paris metro," I say and she grins, knowingly.

For the Want of Cold Water

Nepal – June 2012

As one travels, especially in more remote areas, you get used to there either being no hot water or, in some instances, no water at all. The lodge I was staying at in the Peruvian Amazon, for example, had a generator that only ran for a few hours a day. This meant two things: First, the ceiling fan in my room was mostly for decoration, and second, no hot water. Given the heat and humidity, however, a cold shower was welcomed.

Or there was the time I was making my way to the base camp of Mount Everest through increasingly more remote Tibet where the water went from cold to non-existent. Upon my return, when the water returned, it was cold. As it was also cold outside, I bathed with wet wipes that I borrowed from another traveler for several days. When hot water did return days later and I washed my hair, the descending water resembled chocolate milk.

Lumbini, Nepal, however, is the first time there was no cold water. Admittedly, we were there in summer, which is not the ideal time to visit the area. Our room claimed to have air conditioning, which amounted to a trickle of air coming from a narrow vent nowhere near our beds that was occasionally not hot. Perfect time for a cold shower, however there's only hot water. And not just hot water but scolding hot water. Both taps, sink and shower.

Thinking it might just be a momentary anomaly, I set to rearranging our room so that the bed is under the trickle of not always hot air. But, with the passing of time, it becomes clearer that the water is hot, full stop. So out come the wet wipes and the start of a night sleeping, or more accurately resting, above the sheets.

Around 4 a.m. my wife stirs me to inform me that the water temperature is finally not scolding. Knowing she can tolerate much higher temperatures than myself, I decide to leave the not scolding water to her and return to my restless sleep. Maybe the water will be cooler in the morning. Maybe not.

Stranger on a Train

India – June 2012

It was not supposed to be an overnight train. The distance from Agra to Jaipur is not too far, relatively speaking, and the train was scheduled to get us there before dinner. After waiting two hours on a hot platform with no seating for the train to arrive, it heads off in the wrong direction after it does show up. We stop after an hour in order for an engine to be replaced, which is another two-hour wait. When all is said and done, we'll arrive in Jaipur at 1 a.m.

When we board the train, it's rather full but the small group we're traveling with find space. We're in a sleeper car with three-tier beds and most find places to sleep, though I decide to sit up and keep an eye on our bags as I don't like the look of one passenger in our car, who seems to be eyeing us very carefully. Besides, I never sleep on trains or buses, so it's not like I'm going to lose sleep.

During the slow, hot ride I shut my eyes from time to time and always open them to find the same passenger looking at me. I glance his way and then look back to our bags. Everyone in my group is now asleep, including our guide. He didn't tell us how long of a ride it would be, so I have no idea how far we are from our destination.

Several hours pass before the guy I've been keeping my eye on gets up for his stop. In English, he asks if I'm heading to Jaipur. "Yes," I reply. "It's the next stop," he informs me, "and they don't stop for long." I thank him, sorry to have mistrusted him, and awaken our guide. I let him know what I have learned, and he looks at me as if I'm crazy. He then hops off the train to see what stop we're at and returns in a bit of a panic, realizing I'm correct.

I help him rouse our group as we only have a few minutes until Jaipur. Everyone rushes to wake up and gather their things. It's a mad dash in the middle of the night but we get everyone up and off at the right stop. "How'd you know Jaipur was the next stop?" our guide asks as we head to our hotel. "Lucky guess," I reply, silently thanking the stranger I misjudged.

Pyongyang via Phnom Penh

Cambodia – July 2012

My wife and I are staying with a former colleague of hers in Phnom Penh before heading to Siem Reap for a few days. He has an apartment on the riverfront and a lot of connections, which we use to explore the area as he is working while we're visiting. His evenings are free and for one of them he suggests a nearby North Korean restaurant. Pyongyang Restaurant is a chain of eateries named after the capital of North Korea, with over 100 locations worldwide. The restaurants are owned and operated by a North Korean government organization. As this is probably the closest we'll ever come to visiting North Korea, we give it a go.

The restaurant is unassuming from the outside and its menu includes kimchi dishes, Pyongyang cold noodles, barbecued cuttlefish, and dog meat soup. The prices are relatively high and in U.S. dollars. The staff consists of young Korean women in traditional dress. Our host tells us that they typically work on three-year contracts and are often highly trained graduates of arts colleges. They live above the restaurant and can only go out accompanied by "minders," who ensure they do not attempt to defect.

Unlike China, Japan, Vietnam, and Thailand, whose chopsticks are primarily made of wood or bamboo, Korean chopsticks were traditionally made of iron and today of stainless steel. In addition, Korean chopsticks are typically flat rather than round or square like other Asian cultures. While I consider my chopstick skills to be quite good, I struggle using these. They are heavier and slipperier than I'm used to, which makes eating noodles nearly impossible for this metal chopstick novice. Fortunately, you don't really come here for the food.

After the meal is complete, the servers disappear and the entertainment portion of the night begins. There's a brightly painted backdrop, colored lights, and even glow sticks at one point. Each of the servers is part of the act at one time; our server turns out to be the drummer. I'm getting a particular eighties vibe, especially when one of the women comes out with a keytar. And I'm sure that rhythm pattern is coming from a Casio keyboard from the era.

Photography is not permitted during the performance, and anyone spotted trying to snap a photo during the performance is quickly approached and asked to stop, though we are able to get a photo with our server after the festivities. Having not been to North Korea, I can't say how authentic the meal was, but it's more about the experience here and it was memorable. Now to practice more with those metal chopsticks.

Bhat-less in Bangkok

Thailand – July 2012

Thailand makes up the fourth and final leg of our summer travels this year. A turboprop plane takes us the hour from Siem Reap to Bangkok and then it's more than an hour's drive to our hotel thanks to traffic and the airport being very far out of town. After a bit of a rest, we're off to change some money and have dinner at a recommended restaurant.

The best rate for money exchange is banks, but it's Friday evening and all of the banks are closed and there's not an open money exchange to be found. The ATMs are attached to the banks and access to them seems to be closed as well. We're getting hungry, so we make our way to the recommended restaurant only to find that they are cash only. We try the restaurant next door but they're not sure if they take Mastercard. We continue to keep our eyes out for somewhere to eat (and take Mastercard) when it begins to rain. Fortunately, we spot a bistro that takes the card, so we pop in.

Four flights of stairs later, our three attempts at ordering a Coke and a Sprite result in a bottle of water and my wife's soft-shell crab in curry sauce comes out as fish and chips, which we kindly return. The food, when it arrives correctly, is good but we're still without money and the morning proves to be just as difficult to find an exchange. I finally use an ATM after accepting their 150 Bhat ($5) service fee, not including the 3% fee my bank will charge for a foreign transaction. Who knew it would be this hard to get Thai currency?

Ten days later we return to Bangkok, which continues to be troublesome. We take a taxi to Loha Prasat, a multi-tiered structure with 37 metal spires, signifying the 37 virtues toward enlightenment. It is one of only three such temples in existence, modelled after earlier ones in India and Sri Lanka. Only the taxi driver doesn't drop us off there but instead Wat Suthat, a royal temple of the first grade, one of ten such temples in Bangkok (23 in Thailand). So we explore this temple then walk to the nearby Loha Prasat.

Afterward we try to hail a cab back to our hotel, but all four attempts reach the same result: after showing each driver our hotel's business card, we're told "traffic" and then watch the cab drive away. First, we can't change money, and now we can't get a cab. Rejected, we decided to catch a tuk tuk to the nearest subway station, go two stops, and then walk to our hotel.

Bangkok, you're making it difficult to love you.

It's Not the End of the World as We Know It

Mexico – December 2012

It's December 21, 2012 and we're in San Cristóbal de las Casas, Mexico. Today is the day many say is when the Mayans have prophesied the end of the world. Of course, in reality today marks the end of the previous Mayan calendar and there are no more Maya around to start the next one, but what's a decade without at least one predicted apocalypse? Besides, it's given me a good excuse to come to the Yucatán Peninsula.

It's a rainy day and we've joined a small group heading out to San Juan Chamula, located in the Chiapas highlands, known for its rebels. In fact, we pass truckloads of rebels driving into San Cristobal while we are heading out, replete with masks and rifles and an uncertain purpose. San Juan Chamula enjoys unique autonomous status within Mexico. No outside police or military are allowed in the village as Chamulas has its own police force.

We're dropped off in front of a small cemetery and walk through the rain into the center of town. While visiting their church, home to a unique blend of traditional Maya beliefs with Catholic practices, we are witness to a shaman's sacrifice. None of the locals seem to notice—they pass along to find the altar they are looking for, the one that will hear their prayers. I sit to the side and watch the shaman. He is kneeling, chanting, and rocking gently back and forth all while holding a very passive chicken. After going into a trance-like state, the shaman cleansers the chicken over the smoke from the rows of candles lit in front of him before twisting the bird's neck. The chicken convulses a few times before becoming still and being placed back into the plastic bag it was brought in. After a few more chants, the shaman rises and leaves.

We follow this with a home visit in neighboring San Lorenzo Zinacantán, though this home is also a market and cafeteria. It's good to know that on the last day of the world, after the sacrifices have been made, one can still get in a little shopping.

A Good Night's Sleep

Jordan – March 2013

I have never been much into camping. When I was around ten year's old, my father setup a tent for me and a friend to "camp" in our backyard. Once it was time to sleep, I spent about an hour cold, uncomfortable, and distracted by all the noises of the night, so I left and went to sleep in my room, which was warm, comfortable, and quiet. My opinion of camping has not improved much since then.

Our choice of Jordan came about rather incidentally. Originally the plan was not to travel during my Spring Break but rather to stay home and relax. As the break approached, however, we started to consider a domestic trip. My wife has never been to New Mexico, so I looked into sites, thinking we could situate ourselves in Santa Fe for the week. Then my wife's work required her to attend a conference in Tel Aviv the week before my break, so the plan shifted to us meeting up in Amman after her conference and join a tour of Jordan that perfectly matched my break.

Sometimes travel requires unusual sleeping situations, either out of necessity or for a cultural experience. Over the years we've spent the night in many overnight trains, a few overnight buses, even a yurt in Kyrgyzstan. There have been some home stays and, on rare occasion, some camping. I do my best to avoid this latter option, but nearly any tour of Jordan is going to include a night in a Bedouin-style tent in Wadi Rum. I won't like it, but I will do it.

The day is spent in 4x4s exploring the northern areas of Wadi Rum via an old Roman road. The area is filled with rock bridges and natural rock sculptures. The landscape consists of sandstone mountains and white and pink colored sands. When we arrive at our campsite, we explore the immediate area for a bit before retiring to an elevated enclave in the surrounding rock hills to read and relax for a while. Our shelter for the night is in a single, large, traditional goat hair tent, which is laid out with rugs, mattresses, pillows and sleeping bags.

As night falls, it turns pitch black and we've all taken shelter in the tent. A few chose to take their sleeping out onto the Wadi for the night but the rest remain in the tent. Then someone begins snoring, so more end up outside of the tent. I put in my earplugs and find as comfortable a position as I can on the thin mattress. I'd been dreading this night but then something unexpected happens—I get a good night's sleep.

In the morning, I'm awake and refreshed looking at all of the exhausted expressions of my fellow travelers. None seem to have slept well, neither inside nor outside the tent. My wife had been up most of the night swatting the insects that never bother me. Breakfast is a quiet affair as everyone is still trying to wake up. Me, I'm up for a hike.

Really Putting My Foot in It

Colombia – December 2013

My favorite coffee beans come from Colombia and we're now exploring one of the coffee growing regions of the country. After a tour of a coffee plantation, we're given the option of hiking to a nearby waterfall. We're a small group of five—my wife and myself joined by three single women, all the same age. My wife is more interested in playing with the dogs in the village, so I head off with the women and a young man serving as our guide, who I am soon convinced is half goat.

It's a simple hike to the waterfall, but there is some rock climbing involved to reach it near the end. I take a moment to catch my breath and take in the waterfall. I have to admit I have an issue with waterfalls, or more precisely how they are photographed. While it seems you can never find a landscape photo that wasn't shot at sunrise or sunset, it also seems you can never find a photo of a waterfall that isn't shot without motion blur. Don't get me wrong, they are beautiful photos, just unoriginal and uninspired. While I'm thinking this, one of the women asks me how to get that motion blur you always see in waterfall photos, so I give her a quick lesson on shutter speed but also let her know about the need for a tripod and neutral density filters.

Time at the waterfall over, we're given the choice of taking the simple hike back to town, or a more scenic route. We opt for the scenic route, not realizing it would involve several steep inclines and crossing a bamboo bridge. I'm the last to cross the bridge, which requires a little climbing to get up to. Seems sturdy and not too high. First step on is fine, second step breaks through the bamboo and I'm brought to my knees with one foot dangling beneath the bridge. Our guide, half goat, hops up quickly to help me up. After making sure I'm okay, he tells me that you need to angle your feet when crossing a bamboo bridge. Would have been nice to have known a minute ago.

Having left my mark on the country, or at least one of its bridges, we now begin the inclines and I'm exhausted by the time we make the final approach back to civilization. I'm starting to think about what I'll buy to drink when we arrive when I realize that I'd left my wallet with my wife, figuring I wouldn't need it. One of the women on our tour takes pity on me and loans me enough to buy some orange juice at the first makeshift shop we encounter. When I see my wife again, I let her know about my bridge encounter and she lets me know about all the dogs she's petted.

Fogged Up in Cartagena

Colombia – December 2013

My first experience with humidity came when I was five years old. My maternal grandfather was from Alabama and he, myself, and my mother went back for a visit. I don't quite recollect the humidity myself, though do remember my mother being eaten alive by mosquitos and one of my grandfather's brothers introducing me to chewing tobacco. Years later, when some of my Florida relatives came to visit us in Southern California, I recall my great aunt complaining about the dryness as she applied another layer of lotion and another dose of eye drops.

This native Southern Californian is used to dry heat and doesn't respond well to humidity. As such, I've learned a few tricks when traveling to humid places. First is to wear breathable fabrics. I'll still be miserable but a little less miserable. Next is to use baby powder-based deodorants as regular ones just act like lubricants in high humidity. I also bring aerosol sunscreens since lotions will sit stickily on the skin. Something to wipe away the immense amounts of sweat made from a quick drying fabric is also a necessity as the usual cotton handkerchiefs I carry just turn to soggy messes. But I encountered something new in Cartagena.

We'd been exploring the central part of Colombia for around a week before heading to the Caribbean coastal port city of Cartagena. It is a beautiful, colorful colonial city with cobblestone streets and a lot of humidity. As we enter its walled old town, I take out my camera to start capturing it but notice that the viewfinder is fogged over. No problem, I wipe it with a cloth, but the view is still foggy. Then I notice my lens is fogged over. Not just the lens but also the UV filter I have attached to it. I remove the filter and notice that it's fogged up on both sides, so I put it away and wipe down the lens itself. It's not perfect but better, so I look through the viewfinder again but the world it reveals is still hazy.

I step aside to a courtyard and pop off the lens. The mirror is fogged over and, I'm assuming at this point, so is the sensor. I determine that I have two choices at this point: Figure out how to defog all of these surfaces or take some very atmospheric photos. I ask my wife where nearby she thinks will be air conditioned and she finds a museum only a few yards away. I wander its exhibits with a lens in one hand and my open camera in the other, its mirror exposed to the cool air. Once every surface appears defogged, I give everything a clean and reassemble. The museum has an outdoor patio, so I slowly make my way from the air conditioning into the patio, allowing everything to slowly acclimatize. Everything seems back to normal and photo taking can resume.

After this trip, I do some research and now carry a silica gel packet in my camera bag to prevent, or at least limit, this from happening in the future. Now if I can only figure out how to prevent all of the sweating.

Yes, We Have It, but It Doesn't Work

Uzbekistan – May 2014

This has been a common response throughout Central Asia. Looking for some relief from the heat and ask in a restaurant if they have air conditioning: "Yes, we have it, but it doesn't work." Surprised there's no hot water in the hotel's shower, so you call the front desk to inquire about the hot water: "Yes, we have it, but it doesn't work."

In Tashkent, we're staying the Hotel Uzbekistan, a 17-story monolith of a hotel built in a classic Soviet style. It was once a grand hotel that has fallen into some disrepair, though renovations are underway, and our room is fortunately one of the few that have been renovated. Its reception area is still grand and full service, so I figure this will not be a phrase we come across here. I am correct, though other issues arise.

First, when I head to the hotel's money exchange, the woman assisting me asks, "Are you sure you can spend it all? You can't use it outside of the country." I assure the concerned woman I am traveling with my wife, so I'm spending for two. "But are you sure? You can't spend it outside of the country." I assure her again before she reluctantly hands me a large stack of bills.

It should be noted that at the time, the largest bill in circulation is the 1000 Uzbekistani so'm note, which is worth about 25 cents in U.S. dollars. There is a new 5000 so'm note, worth $1.25, but they are rare. This means that nearly every transaction involves stacks of bills. If you've just exchanged $100 as I have, you end up with four-hundred 1000 so'm notes, which are then divided among several envelopes and assorted hiding places. Every meal has involved at least three currency counts: one by myself, a second count by my wife, and one last count by the waiter or waitress.

The front of the hotel is lined with taxi drivers who don't seem to want to go anywhere. Give them a destination and they either tell you they don't go there or quote an extortionate price and don't seem too upset when you turn them down. This situation is not unique to the hotel. When trying to return from an outing to a distant madrasa, not one taxi stops for us as we try to flag them from the street. Fortunately, a local pulls over and asks where we're headed and quotes a reasonable price back to our hotel.

At the airport, I point to rows of Russian "Coke" behind the shopkeeper and ask for a cola. "No cola, only tea or water," I am told. The year before, Coca-Cola disappeared from the shelves in Uzbekistan due to a scandal involving a company linked to the president's daughter, though Russian substitutes can be found. I then head to a bar where I can grab a Pepsi and use up some remaining Uzbekistani so'm and am told: "Sorry, no so'm. Only euros or dollars." Don't tell the woman at the hotel I'm going to be leaving the country with a few so'm left over or she make not give any to the next guest looking to exchange money.

Don't Worry, There is No Flesh

Philippines – March 2014

Ifugao Provence is named after the Ifugao people that live in the mountainous region of north-central Luzon around the of town Banaue. They are former headhunters who are renowned for their stunning mountain-hugging rice terraces. The Ifugao are believed to have arrived from China around 2000 years ago. Their first contact with the outside world was through American military officers and schoolteachers early in the 20th century, when the Philippines was a U.S. colony. Communication with them was made easier when better roads were built to the areas where they live.

The Banaue Rice Terraces were carved into the mountains by the ancestors of the indigenous people. It is thought that the terraces were built with minimal equipment, largely by hand. They are fed by an ancient irrigation system from the rainforests above the terraces. It is said that if the steps were put end to end, they would encompass half of the globe. Locals still plant rice and vegetables on the terraces, although many younger Ifugaos do not find farming appealing, instead opting for the more lucrative hospitality industry generated by the terraces.

We've come to Banaue via an overnight sleeper bus from Manila. The bus is so packed that one can't recline and it's also blaring air conditioning throughout the night. I suppose locals may be able to sleep, but it's not in the cards for me. As we've arrived early, we drop our bags off at our hotel before heading into town for some breakfast and exploration of the terraces. After breakfast, we take a tuk tuk to the top of a hill and then start a slow walk down, giving us close-up views of the terraces and local life in the area. We head back to our hotel in the afternoon, now able to check-in, shower, and rest a while.

In the morning, we follow a trail behind our hotel that leads into an Ifugao village. On the way down the steep and narrow trail, we come across a small shop selling textiles and wood carvings. Here I find a Bulul, a carved wooden figure used by the Ifugao to guard rice crops. The non-souvenir sculptures are highly stylized representations of ancestors and are thought to gain power from the presence of the ancestral spirit. Mine is coming home with me to guard other souvenirs on a shelf.

Further down we arrive at the village proper. Along with their extensive rice terraces, the Ifugao also have a distinct way of remembering their dead. Six years after a body is buried, the bones are dug up, after which a celebration takes place. This ritual is repeated one more time after another six years. Sometimes the Ifugao invite tourists to see the bones of their ancestors. This is what happened to us, or at least to my wife, who can't watch any movies involving ghosts or hauntings.

While we are wandering around the village, a lady comes up to my wife while I am taking some photographs. She asks if my wife would like to see the bones of her ancestor. My wife is hesitant in her response as she is taken aback by the offer. "Don't worry," the woman responds to my wife's hesitation, "there is no flesh on the bones." My wife respectfully declines, and we take this as our cue to leave before any more bones are offered.

Checkpoint Smuggling

Bolivia – December 2014

We've just finished a tour of Bolivia and find ourselves back in La Paz with two free days. This trip was my wife's first experience in altitude and they didn't get along, but she seems acclimatized now. For our first free day we explore the city, including a cable car ride to a lookout point and a visit to the Witches' Market. We also head out to the nearby Valley of the Moon. For our second day, we have no plans, so we head to the travel agent attached to our hotel and explore our options.

Many years ago, I was in Peru and near the end of my trip spent a few days in and around Lake Titicaca. As I always like to see both sides of sights that reside in two countries, like Iguassu Falls (Argentina and Brazil) or Victoria Falls (Zambia and Zimbabwe), we decide on a day trip out to the Bolivian side of Lake Titicaca. Many of our travel friends who have seen both sides highly recommend the Bolivian side. As one friend put it, "Bolivia gets the titi, while Peru gets the caca."

It's a three-hour bus ride from La Paz to the lake and around two-and-a-half hours in, we come to a river. In order to cross it, everyone disembarks so that the bus can be driven onto a vehicle ferry while passengers board a commuter ferry. It seems a bit complicated for a five-minute crossing, but there are bigger concerns to address. As we start to get off the bus, we're told to bring our passports, as this is a checkpoint. We're crossing from Bolivia to Bolivia, so I'd never thought to bring our passports and the travel agent didn't tell us.

I catch our local guide and explain the situation. He thinks for a minute then tells us to stay on the bus as they never check inside the bus. If they do check and find some stowaways without identification? Not to worry, he assures us, they never check the bus. So, we duck down in our seats and cross using our senses. Sounds like we've driven onto the ferry. Now it feels like we are floating in the right direction. Five minutes later, we slow and dock. Then the driver reappears to take the bus off the ferry. We've successfully crossed from Bolivia to Bolivia without passports.

Personally, I prefer the Peruvian side of the lake, even though that visit did not require being smuggled across a checkpoint. On our way back, I ask our guide if we need to stay on the bus again when crossing back over the river. "No," he says, "they don't check passports going this direction." I'm still not sure why they check passports going the other direction, but don't want to dive into the bureaucracy.

Monkey Versus Monkey

Nicaragua – March 2015

Lake Nicaragua is the largest lake in Central America and includes more than 300 tiny tropical islands, which were formed more than 10,000 years ago when Mombacho Volcano erupted. We're staying in Granada and have a boat tour of the lake booked this morning, culminating in a stop on one of the islands, owned and operated by a French couple. In fact, it's their daughter who comes to pick us up from our hotel and take us to our boat.

After around an hour cruising the lake and seeing many views of Mombacho Volcano, we land on our island and am greeted by the owner's wife, who somehow looks effortlessly glamourous in the heat and humidity. She guides us to a rest area near the middle of the island, where her husband is there to greet us and introduce us to Cashew, a capuchin monkey. Cashew doesn't seem too interested in me, but it drawn to my wife. I'm assuming it's either her ponytail or the fact that in the Chinese zodiac she's also a monkey.

When Cashew is with the husband, he's rather well behaved. It's after the husband has given us a tour of the small island that Cashew's true nature appears. My wife and I are lounging under some trees on the shore when we hear some distant rustling. The rustling grows louder when suddenly Cashew lands on my wife and starts playing with her ponytail. She's able to snap a quick selfie with him on her phone but, once the phone is put away, he starts to gently attack her arms. As my wife tries to calm him, he starts to bite. Not hard but enough for my wife to push him away, which seemed to mean playtime for Cashew.

We're then called for some refreshments by the owner, who reclaims the monkey. While we're eating our fruit, Cashew is on his best behavior and sits beside me patiently while I hand him some fruit, which he eats in peace. Once the snack is over, he's back on my wife who starts spinning with him hanging on to her arm to try to release him. I shoot a quick video, figuring I can use it for future blackmail. The husband returns to check on us and Cashew runs to him, gentle as can be.

We're back to lounging by the water. It's peaceful for a few minutes, but then the rustling starts up again and my wife tenses up. We look into the branches trying to find the monkey and neither of us see his return, immediately clinging to my wife's arm and attacking her ponytail. Soon he's back to the gentle biting and she's back to the spinning. I assist by shooting another video.

Irish Karma

Ireland – July 2015

In Ireland, it's believed fairy trees are the sacred grounds for the *sídhe*, better known as the little people or the wee folk and most often portrayed as fairies. A fairy tree is usually a Hawthorn or an Ash tree that stands alone in fields and are commonly found with large stones circling its base, most likely to protect it. With fairy trees being regarded as sacred sites for the wee folk, there are many superstitions surrounding them, several involving magic and bad luck. Some believe if you damage or cut down one of these trees, you'll be faced with a life of bad luck.

We're heading back to Dublin after a tour around Ireland when our guide mentions that the highway we're on had to be redirected during construction as there was a particularly beloved fairy tree that was in its original path and the locals protested its removal. The redirection cost millions of dollars, which my wife scoffs at. "It's just a tree," she notes.

When we arrive at our hotel a few hours later, she starts to not feel well. We rest in the room a bit before dinner and eat at the hotel to stay close to our room. The rest and food don't help and she's back in bed soon after. I edit some photos and research a route to take the following day to get in some good sites as our tour is now over and it's a free day that also happens to be my birthday.

In the morning she's still feeling off, so I look up the nearest pharmacy and head out on foot to get her some medicine. Upon my return, she's still in bed, so I leave her to rest, put out a Do Not Disturb sign, and head off for some nearby sightseeing, periodically checking my phone for a text or email from her. I head back to the hotel around lunch time, but she's not up for food, so I head back out for lunch and a bit more sightseeing.

I don't know if it was the tree or a fairy she offended, but the offense only seemed to last twenty-four hours as she's out of bed and ready for dinner when I return. I'd booked us an after-dinner tour that involves two actors performing scenes and passages from the work of Samuel Beckett while also visiting some of Dublin's most noted pubs. He's my favorite playwright and I have an affinity for both Guinness and Irish whiskey, so it seemed like a good pairing. Surprisingly she's up for it, though I think we'll take it slow and skip the alcohol for her.

Seven-Star High Tea

United Arab Emirates – December 2015

Dubai's Burj Al Arab (Tower of Arabs) is often called the world's only seven-star hotel, though officially the star rating for hotels only goes to five. Going by the official rating, it would still need to go above five. One of the tallest hotels in the world, the Burj Al Arab has 28 double-story floors that accommodate a total of 202 suites, the smallest of which is larger than my first house. The hotel has a shuttle service with Rolls-Royces and a helicopter, and is home to six restaurants, one of which is accessed via a simulated submarine voyage. Suites start around $2000 a night and go upwards of $24,000, though this includes a butler and private chef.

Though Chinese, my wife was raised in London and has acquired a love of high tea. As my mother's side of the family is British, I enjoy it as well, though find the American version lacking and overpriced. High tea is meant to be a treat of tea, sandwiches, scones, and cake, while American high tea tends to skip the sandwiches or replace them with salads. No high tea should ever be served with salad. We have had some exception high teas in London, and I have started seeking them out when we travel. When I found out that Burj Al Arab offers high tea, I was quick to book as it should be both remarkable and the only way we'd ever be allowed in the place.

Clearly, we're not the only ones into high tea as the group we've joined is rather large and international. Our bus is stopped before the turn to the manmade island that holds the hotel and our guide has to show a rather hefty folder to a security guard. Across the bridge and it's the same on the other side. Once inside the hotel, he's off with his folder to speak with someone at the front desk. The hotel's lobby is grand and ornate, with long pillars of gold shooting up the sail-like structure of the building. I take a few photos while trying not to look too much like a tourist. Then again, half the people in the lobby seem to be taking photos, so it's not like I'll stick out.

After a short wait, our group is escorted up very long escalators to the elevators. We're broken into smaller groups and escorted up to the top floor, where our restaurant is located. We're asked to stay on this floor until our tea is over and we're summoned back down. I suppose if I was spending thousands a night, I wouldn't want commoners wandering the floors either. From the top floor restaurant, one can look straight down, which is a sea of deep blue carpets and ornate wooden doors.

As we've only just met, everyone in our group is rather reserved, but we're in such a beautiful location that my wife offers to take photos of couples and groups with their elegant tea settings. I use this time to explore a bit of the floor we're on, trying to get in a few photos before our minder comes back to escort us down to the lobby and out of the hotel. As I get near the elevators, there's an attendant keeping an eye on me. No worries, I just return to our tea and pretending we belong.

Christmas in Qatar

Qatar – December 2015

I've always enjoyed traveling during the holidays as it saves me from figuring out how to celebrate them when at home. It can also bring about some memorable experiences. It was during a celebration in Peru on Christmas Eve that I learned I have a high tolerance for vodka and my hotel in Tunisia went all out on another Christmas Eve, with a seven-course meal and band straight out of the eighties in their choice of music. It felt more like a prom than a Christmas party, though I appreciated the effort.

We arrive in Doha, Qatar's capital, on Christmas day and the only sense of the season is that it's raining—snow would be too much to ask for. We take a taxi from the airport to our hotel, which is more like an apartment. We've just come from something similar in Dubai, though our accommodations there included two bedrooms, two bathrooms, a kitchen, living room, and dining area. If we'd known anyone in the area, I would have thrown a party just to use the space. In Doha we've been downsized to a more sensible single bedroom and bathroom, living area and kitchen.

It's getting late and the rain hasn't let up. Our hotel doesn't have a restaurant, so I do some online investigation and discover a Yemeni option just a block from where we're staying. Only problem is, we weren't expecting rain in this part of the world and neither of us have packed an umbrella. We ask at the front desk before departing and they offer us one, which we promise to return.

We walk slowly to the restaurant as the ground is rather saturated. It's a large umbrella and covers us both. As we find the entrance to the restaurant, I happen to look back toward our hotel only to find we've been followed the whole time by an employee. Seems we have their only umbrella and he followed us to make sure to return it in case another guest needs it. Here's hoping the rain lets up by the time we're ready to return.

Yemen is high on our travel list, but this will be the closest we're going to come for the foreseeable future. If the country is as amazing as the food, we're certainly missing out. The restaurant has an open seating area and a more private section, which is where all the families and groups with women are seated behind curtained booths. This is the area we're taken to and, with the curtain closed around our table, our friendly waiter starts to bring us bottled water and the most delicious meat in a flavorful broth. Yemeni dishes are often comprised of meat and bones either stewed, grilled, or boiled in soups, which suits us perfectly.

Merry Christmas to us!

Grounded by Air Force One

Cuba – March 2016

My wife has a British passport, so she's been to Cuba before as there are no restrictions on her travels there. I have a U.S. passport, which is a bit more complicated. So, when travel for Americans became available through cultural people-to-people tours, I jumped at the opportunity. We'd be meeting our group in Miami before taking a chartered flight to Havana and, at the end of the tour, another chartered flight from Havana back to Miami. What I didn't realize when I booked the tour was that our return flight was scheduled two hours before President Obama was to touch down in Havana.

I figured with a two-hour departure time before the president's arrival, there shouldn't be any issues. Then our flight is delayed. About an hour later, we are called to board and ushered onto a bus that takes us across the tarmac to our plane. Then we sit there, well actually stand there, for twenty minutes. We're then driven back to the terminal. All entries and exits to the airport are then closed and locked as Air Force One is soon to land.

I shouldn't have wanted to depart as being in the airport and witnessing the locals' reactions was incomparable. Terminal screens are tuned to news coverage and we are soon watching Air Force One land on the same tarmac we had just been on. Everyone is watching attentively, some taking photos and videos with their phones. I do the same with my aging iPhone. After the plane comes to a halt and President Obama makes his first appearance from the main hatch, cheers ring out in the terminal. The atmosphere is hopeful and a little festive—this is a Latin American country, after all.

All during our stay, the changing political climate had been the talk. Even during our guided tour of Old Havana with a local architect, he had mentioned that should a company such as Starbucks wish to purchase a prime location, his hope was that a deal could be reached so that they could revitalize more than just the property they were interested in. While the Cubans wanted American business, they also knew that American business wanted Cuba and were willing to exploit that. It might not be capitalism, but it's a close cousin.

Not So Happy Birthday to Me

Jamaica – July 2016

I decide to splash out for my birthday, even though it's not a milestone year. I found a deal on Business Class tickets, which I figured would allow us the use of the airline's lounge. Instead of booking at a large resort outside of town filled with fellow tourists, which isn't really our style, we went with one in Montego Bay proper where the locals tend to stay. And we'd be arriving on my birthday. So far so good.

The night before we're flying out, I start to feel off. This is the third time this has happened to me the past year, the last time being the day of our flight from Taiwan to Hong Kong. I know it will pass as it's allergy related but the timing is not good. I figure we have a shuttle to the airport and a lounge awaiting us, so it shouldn't be too bad. Only the lounge is not awaiting us. When I present our tickets, I'm told our destination is not international enough to allow us access, even though it's Business Class.. Fine, at least it's going to be a comfortable flight.

While the flight was fine, it landed us around 8 a.m. and the resort doesn't start checking guests in until 3 p.m. Knowing this, I booked a sightseeing tour around the area that picks us up at 10 a.m. and returns us around 1 p.m. We drop our bags at the hotel and wait in the lobby for our guide to arrive. When he does, he drives us around for about an hour, never stopping, and then we're back at the hotel. Still four hours to go. I check in at the front desk to see if there's any chance of getting into the room early, even 2 p.m. would work, and they say they'll let me know.

It's a hot and humid lunch at the hotel's outdoor restaurant. Then it's back to the small lobby area, which is air conditioned. It's noon and becoming increasingly clear there is going to be no early check in, so we make ourselves at home. If I were feeling better, we'd explore the town below us, but I'd rather save my strength for the remainder of the trip. Somehow, we make it to 3 p.m. and can finally check in.

Our room is nice, though there's only air conditioning in the bedroom, rendering the seating area and kitchen uninhabitable in the heat. I check the bathroom to discover there is no soap or shampoo. I call the front desk to be told that they consider our rooms apartments, so those items are not included. We drop off our bags and head into town looking for soap and shampoo. We usually bring them along but didn't this time, figuring a "resort" would provide them.

I have the great fortune of usually being avoided by insects, especially mosquitos. My mom was a magnet for them as is my wife, but for some reason they tend to leave me alone. It's not until we return from our shopping trip that I discover there's something in Jamaica that hasn't gotten the memo about me as my elbows and ankles are now filled with swollen and itchy bites. So, I slather on the anti-itch cream, turn on the air conditioning, and hope to sleep the rest of my birthday away.

Never Judge a Church by Its Exterior

El Salvador – March 2017

Plaza Libertad, or Freedom Square, is located in the historic center of the city of San Salvador and it was from here that the expansion of the city began in the middle of the 16th century. Notably, Plaza Libertad is the only plaza in the entire historic center of San Salvador that has retained its location since its creation around the year 1545, where the independence struggle of all Central America began.

We're here with a local guide to explore and see the sights. There are still some colonial buildings to be found, though they share a similarly rundown quality to those found in Havana. While we're wandering the area, I notice what appears to be a derelict building in a prime spot along the main square. I figure it must have once been important based on its location and snap a quick photo as I like its brutalist design.

To my surprise, when we return to this location, we head toward this building. Benjamin, our guide, says he'd like to show us what he considers to be the highlight of this city tour. I know he knows I like photography and we've already explored some photogenic ruins together, but this one seems an odd choice. But he hasn't led us astray in three days together, so we follow him.

Designed by sculptor Ruben Martinez and completed in 1971, Iglesia El Rosario (Rosario Church) is profoundly beautiful inside. Its nondescript concrete exterior conceals an arched roof and a rainbow of natural light rushing across the altar and bouncing off the metal and rock. The colors are amazing, providing a full spectrum of light about the space. I setup my camera for low light shooting and warn Benjamin that we're going to be here a while.

Compared to other churches throughout Central America that follow the Latin and Greek cross structure, Rosario has no pillars that obstruct the visibility of the faithful toward the altar and the multihued light adds a dramatic quality to the religious images inside. For me, Rosario is only rivalled by Managua's New Cathedral and, even then, one's eye is attracted more by the modern architectural elements, whereas here one is well aware they are in a religious location.

I do the best I can photographing inside without a tripod and without disturbing the occasional attendee who comes in through a side entrance to sit among this incredible site. As we leave, I complement Benjamin on his seemingly questionable choice. "Guests always are surprised," he replies. I certainly was.

Art Underground

Sweden – May 2017

We're in Stockholm for a few days while on our way to Rome, where we're going to join friends for a week. Fortunately, we've already gotten some sightseeing in as today it's raining. Not to worry, as we've planned a tour of the Stockholm subway system.

Over 90 of the 100 subway stations in Stockholm have been decorated with sculptures, mosaics, paintings, installations, engravings, and reliefs by over 150 artists. One subway station, for instance, looks like an archaeological excavation, with the "remains" of an old Stockholm palace. At another station, a local artist used the space to highlight women's rights and environmental issues.

My wife has already looked up which stations we can easily reach from our nearest station, so we head out in the rain and begin our makeshift tour. We purchase a day pass and have planned a route that keeps us underground and out of the rain. It's also after the morning rush, so few people are on the trains or at the stations, which is good for exploration and photography. I start by shooting in color but realize that some black and white would also look good, and I could use the limited number of travelers to accent my shots—street photography under the streets.

We begin in T-Centralen Station, typically one of Stockholm's busiest, which features the work of Per Olof Ultvedt covering the white cave-like walls with beautiful blue leaves. Just a few stops from T-Centralen is Stadion Station, which features pale blue walls and a rainbow archway that is positioned between two platforms. It's here that I get my idea to shoot some in black and white and also end up with one of my favorite photos of the trip.

The station of Solna Centrum features a bright green and red landscape, the green symbolizing the forest and the red an evening sun setting behind the treetops. Originally the walls were supposed to be only green and red but, after completing the walls, artists Karl-Olov Björk and Anders Åberg felt they were lacking. So they continued adding various details and scenes to the forest, which were mostly improvised.

Kungsträdgården Station is a surreal mix of checkered floor, red and green striped patterns, some random sculptures and ceiling graphics. While the station is meant to mimic its above ground namesake, one of Stockholm's oldest public parks, its wild design and use of complementary colors reminds me more of an Alice in Wonderland inspired hallucination.

We resurface in the early afternoon to find the rain has subsided, so we're able to find a nice place to eat and do some above ground exploring. I make the mistake of looking up several of the stations we didn't see and find some incredible ones, such as Odenplan, whose entrance features a "lifeline" of fluorescent lights modelled from the heartbeat of the artist's son. Guess we'll have something to return to if we ever find ourselves in Stockholm again.

Roaming in Rome

Italy – June 2017

The first trip my future wife and I took together was to the Western Balkans, which was completed using only public transport and started off in a rented apartment in Dubrovnik, Croatia. This was years before services like Airbnb were available, so communication with the owner was done via direct email and payment was made on arrival in cash. When we arrived at the airport and I handed the taxi driver the address, he didn't seem to know where it was. This led to me using my cellphone to call the owner, who then spoke with the driver to give him directions and the two of them then chatted on our way to the apartment, all the while my cell was racking up roaming charges by the minute.

I am reminded of this experience many years later in Rome, where we are sharing an apartment with friends. They often come to Rome and invited us to join them. I'm someone who tends to avoid staying at other people's homes and has never had a roommate, but the price and location were right, and it turns out there was nothing to worry about as we kept very different schedules. My wife and I like to leave early to avoid the afternoon heat, then cool off somewhere for lunch before heading back out. We'll return to our room in the late afternoon for some rest before heading out again to find somewhere for dinner along with some nighttime sightseeing. Our friends, on the other hand, prefer to head out in the afternoon and stay out late, so we hardly ever encountered each other in the apartment. The only overlap is putting out laundry to dry on the patio furniture.

Our shared apartment is just off the Piazza del Popolo (People's Square), by the city's northern gate. We're walking distance from Villa

Borghese, Trevi Fountain, and the Spanish Steps, and our close vicinity allows us to visit before the rush of day trippers. We're also near a metro station that can easily take us to Palatine Hill, the center-most of the Seven Hills of Rome and one of the most ancient parts of the city. It stands 130 feet above the Roman Forum, looking down upon it on one side and upon Circus Maximus on the other. From the time of Augustus, Imperial palaces were built here and consequently it became the etymological origin of the word "palace."

More public transport takes us to Vatican City, though the crowds here have already gathered and there's a long line of people waiting in the sun to enter St. Peter's Basilica, so I opt to photograph them instead of joining them. It's a taxi ride to MAXXI, or the National Museum of the 21st Century Arts, a museum of contemporary art and architecture in the Flaminio quartiere. It was designed as a multidisciplinary space by Zaha Hadid and is committed to experimentation and innovation in the arts and architecture. We thought it would be nice to include some modern architecture among the ancient ruins. Rome really is an open-air museum and this photographer is very happy.

When we were first discussing sharing an apartment, one of our friends did ask me with some concern if we'd want to spend all of our time together. I told her no, we'd do our own things, though could meet up for dinner if we were both free. That only happened once, our first night in Rome, and only because a delayed flight caused us to both arrive at the airport, and subsequently the apartment, at the same time. I was able to order one of the last fried artichokes of the season before my wife and I headed back to the apartment to sort our things after our flight, and our friends headed out for their first of many late nights out.

Museo a Cielo Abierto

Chile – March 2018

I gained an appreciation for graffiti and street art a few summers ago in London. It started with a graffiti tour with a local artist that took us to Brick Lane, which provided some history and context. This led to looking up some other areas about London known for their street art and purchasing the work of some of these artists for our house when we returned home. Now we look up street art when we travel, seeing what's nearby and worth a visit.

This is true for a free day in Santiago. I found a tour with a company that will run its tours with even just one person, and we are pleasantly surprised when we meet our guide that it's just her and us. We head to the metro and on to San Miguel, where the Museo a Cielo Abierto is located, which is Chile's largest street art collective. Meaning "Open Air Museum," the museo is a vibrant collection of murals that transforms an often-unexplored area into a blossoming outdoor art gallery.

In the 1960s, the neighborhood was built for working class people who moved into the area while it was rapidly expanding. The people who lived here endured poverty and the political turmoil that arose after a 1973 coup. Years of pollution and neglect left many of the houses in rough shape. In 2009, two locals had the idea to use street art to refresh the buildings and bring new life to the neighborhood. The first mural was unveiled in 2010. Now, more than forty line the streets, each one becoming an artistic backdrop to everyday life.

Along with revitalization, the project also aims to educate, featuring murals that deal with themes such as workers' rights in Chile, and to involve the residents of the neighborhood, who have input in approving the sketches of the murals. The artists involved in this project are diverse in their backgrounds, styles, and nationalities. Local artists from Santiago and regional artists from the south of Chile share the streets with international artists from other countries in South America and in Europe.

Our tour over, we head back to Santiago and share a drink with our guide at a local cafe. We mention we're headed to Easter Island in two days and she lights up. Turns out she lived there for nine months and provides us a list of places to see and some to avoid. "Overpriced," she warns us of one restaurant. "Tacky," she tells us of another. She's also heading to Europe in the fall, so we offer her some do's and don'ts of our own.

Intel exchanged, our guide orders us an Uber and we're soon back to our hotel. We'll be back staying at the same hotel when we return from Easter Island, which turned out to be a good call as the only flight out is delayed hours due to maintenance issues and most with connecting flights will end up missing their connections. We're instead able to skip the stress and grab a taxi to our hotel, where our room is upgraded and I'm also able to get a late checkout before returning to the airport the following afternoon.

An Unwelcoming Welcome

Haiti – July 2018

We've been making our way over the past few days north from Santo Domingo in the Dominican Republic to the border town of Dajabón, which will be our crossing into Haiti and on to Cap-Haïtien for the next few days. Twice a week the town also serves as a massive market and we happen to be here on one of these days. The market is completely fenced in from the rest of the Dominican Republic and the road out of Dajabón has numerous military checkpoints to prevent Haitians from entering the country. Most of what the Haitians sell are used clothes and shoes, bulk dry goods, and housewares.

We meet our Haitian guide and driver at the Dominican side of the border after exiting the country, and they drive us across the bridge over the Massacre River to Ouanaminthe, where entering the country is a much simpler and less hectic affair. We're on the road for about twenty minutes before we come across our first Haitian checkpoint and our SUV is asked to pull over. An already agitated and well-armed officer comes to speak to our driver and guide. My wife grows uneasy as his rifle is on her side of the vehicle, pointed at her window. As they converse, his agitation increases, and he soon asks for our passports. We've made it twenty minutes before running into trouble.

The officer heads over to another official sitting in the shade, so I'm assuming he's the one in charge. He hands him our passports and they speak for a while. Time passes. Our guide is young and seemed to be arguing with the agitated officer earlier, which is never a good idea, so we are pleased to see that our driver, who is far more even-tempered, is the one to leave the vehicle and go speak with the one in charge.

More time passes. Our driver finally returns with our passports and we're back on the road.

"Is this a common occurrence?" we ask our guide. "You never know," he says. "There are lots of checkpoints and it depends on their mood." Welcome to Haiti.

A Second Honeymoon

Namibia – December 2018

Namibia is a very large country with very bad roads. It's summer and we're in an adventure truck with no air conditioning and I'm betting no shock absorbers. It's been a long, hot, and bumpy ride from our supply stop in Springbok, South Africa, to our destination for the night, a camp on the banks of the Orange River. The accommodations are split into two sets, one along the river and one higher, overlooking the river. Our room number indicates we're situated above the river, so after checking in we're taken up to the start of the rooms overlooking the river.

We're left to drag our bags along a dirt road to find our room. First problem is that, while our key has a room number on it, the rooms themselves appear to have names and not numbers. I then notice that if you go right up to the front door, there is a small number. After a few sightings of the small numbers, I notice the numbers are increasing. We start at ten and our room is seventeen, so it should just be a few rooms up. However, we run out of rooms after sixteen.

There appears to be a few more rooms beyond a pit with a very small path across it on one side. I leave my wife at room sixteen with our bags as I carefully make it across the pit and on to the other side. At first these rooms don't appear to have numbers or names and I soon realize this is because they are not rooms but rather offices. So I make my way back along the narrow path along the pit and we start to walk back toward the reception area. Fortunately, someone else has just been driven up to their room and we inquire with the driver about our room. Oh, that's along the river, we're told, so it's bags back in the van and a drive to the other set of rooms.

Now that I know where the numbers are, I see we're starting with one. Not quite sure where seventeen is located considering ten through sixteen are on the other side of the property, but we keep at it. Five, six, seven, then seventeen. Of course, why didn't I think of that? I'm thinking maybe it's some sort of play on one plus seven makes eight until I notice that the next cabin is number eight. What sort of strange math is this?

It's then that we notice our cabin appears to be twice the size of all the others we have passed. Turns out, we're in the honeymoon suite, complete with a full sitting area inside and a very large patio outside overlooking the Orange River. I'm assuming now that it's a recent addition and, as there wasn't room after sixteen, it was placed where there was room between cabins seven and eight. Then I tell my analytical side to be quiet as I start to close the blinds of the windows that makeup three of the four walls so that the air conditioning can get to work. I want to make sure we're refreshed for the sunset that should be spectacular from our private patio.

Delta Glamping

Botswana – December 2018

We've been in Namibia for about two weeks and I'm ready to move on. Not that I haven't enjoyed the country and its beautiful sights, I am just feeling the itch for something new. At least I was until we come to our accommodation for our first night in Botswana, and then I wish I was back in Namibia. Even Dickens couldn't have imagined a place this despairing when he was describing the slums of London.

So, we're very happy to be on our way the following morning, catching a flight to the Okavango Delta. When we get to our plane, it's small, holding two pilots, my wife and I, and our day packs. We wonder why there are two pilots when we notice that there is nothing modern about this plane and the co-pilot seems to be there to navigate by compass and landmarks. It's a low and turbulent flight that my wife hates, though I enjoy immensely. There are not too many planes you can photograph out the window of and capture both a wing and a wheel.

We land on one of the many small airstrips along the delta, each owned by a different campsite or lodge. It's then on to a boat as our campsite is further in. We're greeted at the port and then it hits me that we'll be camping. Based upon the accommodations the night before, I begin to wonder what fresh hell we may be in for. I shouldn't have worried though, as we've risen from hell to heaven.

Our "tent" is spacious and set on the banks of Weboro Lagoon, offering panoramic views from our private deck. The tent is light and airy and has an en-suite bathroom with a large rain shower head. The bathroom is adjoined to the room by a short corridor, which provides another view over the lagoon. We are warned that there's a monkey who has learned when dinner is and, while guests are off enjoying their meals, he comes to the tents to see who has left one unlocked for him to rummage through. We make sure to lock the door on our way to dinner, which is even better than the tent, providing one of the best meals we've had this trip.

In the morning we're off for a cruise of the delta, then back for lunch, and off again for an afternoon boat ride. We're resting in our tent when we hear a rustling at the door. It seems the monkey is either early or we're running late for dinner, though either way he's not happy to see the tent is locked and occupied. After another excellent meal, we're not happy to be leaving in the morning.

A Slow Crossing

Zimbabwe – December 2018

We're told to get to the Zimbabwe border early as it can get rather busy. It opens at 7 a.m., so we're up early and on our way to arrive before 8 a.m. There are a number of buildings at the border, but we make our way to the one for visitors requiring a visa. We're in need of KAZA Visas, which allows for unlimited entries and exits between Zimbabwe and Zambia, where we plan to pop into in a few days. However, this type of visa can only be acquired at the border and they have been known to run out.

We're one of the first in line, though there's no one else around. I confirm that the border opens at 7 a.m. and stare at the locked doors and windows of the building before us. Around 8:15 a.m., three officials approach our building, enter, and open three of the windows. Now we'll get moving, I think. With three windows open, they should be able to quickly accommodate the growing number of people behind us. Only this is not the case. First, it's after 8:30 a.m. that the officials start to work. Second, everyone must visit the middle window to be processed, one at a time. If they need a typical tourist visa, they then move to the window on the left; if they need a KAZA Visa, then they move to the window on the right. At least this gives me hope that they have KAZA Visas.

Once the process starts, I time how long it takes to process someone, which seems to be around ten minutes. I learn why when it's my turn. The middle official needs to complete a third-page form that is then given to one of the officials on either side of him. When I'm up, he had just completed the third of three forms on the prior page, so now he flips to a new page and carefully positions a piece of carbon paper between it and the duplicate form below. Once everything is lined up, he takes my passport and begins to complete my form. He writes slowly and deliberately, and, when finished, very slowly tears the form along the perforated lines. Once the form is free, he lifts the carbon paper and checks that every letter and number from the top form has been copied exactly to the form below. I'm beginning to miss the German efficiency of Namibia.

As I've asked for a KAZA Visa, my form is passed to the official on the right. It's been a while since someone has asked for this type of visa, so now this official needs to re-setup shop. He slowly looks over my form to verify that I do indeed need a KAZA Visa, then takes out a spool of stickers and carefully removes one to then carefully place into my passport. He writes in some of the information from my form on the visa and then slowly stamps my new visa. He checks my form again to confirm that I had already paid the other official, then hands me my passport with visa affixed. I think I'm done but it's also possible I've fallen asleep and am having a bad dream. Then again, that probably requires a different form completed in triplicate.

Here Staircase, Staircase

England – June 2019

On our-second-to-last day in London, we set about exploring some areas we had not gotten to before heading off on our Albania, Kosovo, and North Macedonia trip. One site I particularly want to explore is Tate Modern. I've seen two locations within the gallery on Instagram I'd like to try my hand at: the tall, slit windows that cast a striking reflection on the cement floor near one of the entrances, and the spiral staircase.

The slit windows are easy to find and, while it's a cloudy day without the sun's rays creating the arresting reflection, I see what I can do. These days Instagram inspirations tend to motivate copying but I'm more interested in seeing what I can do differently. Besides, I've always liked a challenge. After a while spent shooting from different angles and heights, I set off to find the spiral staircase.

After perusing a few floors, I come to the realization that I have no idea where it is. I connect to Tate's wifi and see someone tagging the location as Tate Library, which causes a minor panic. Am I in the wrong place? Where is the Tate Library? Why am I panicking when everyone else tags it as Tate Modern? Who is this nitwit tagging it as Tate Library?

Mild panic over, I try a new approach: If I were designing the gallery and wanted to put in a spiral staircase, where would I put it? Answer: the ground floor. So, I head back down to the ground floor and this time, not being distracted by the slit windows, easily find the staircase. Most images I've seen include a solo person in a prime spot in a well composed shot, though I sometimes suspect it's the photographer's spouse or friend. I focus more on images without people as I'm more interested in the shadows and curves.

It's taken me longer than it should have to have taken these photos and I'm sure my wife is wondering what became of me. Then again, she's in the gift shop and probably in no great hurry to leave.

Losing My Seat in London

England – June 2019

It's our last day in London and we've come to Kingston for my wife and her mother to hit the sales and for me to find a coffee shop for a few hours. Before this, we head to John Lewis, as they have a laptop and watch I'd like to look at before ordering them online upon our return. I'd seen them there a few weeks earlier but didn't inspect them as carefully as I'd now like to. We set a time to meet and I head toward electronics.

I strike out as they now have neither the laptop nor watch I am interested in, so after aimlessly wandering for a bit (and with about fifteen minutes before out meeting time), I head to the downstairs Waitrose as it's cool and my favorite supermarket in the U.K. My exploration quickly done, I notice a bench at the end of the registers and sit to check my email.

A few minutes before I am scheduled to meet my wife and mother-in-law, I hear a voice behind me say, "I don't suppose you are going to be leaving any time soon?" It takes a second to realize that the question is being addressed to me. I turn to see a very old woman behind me who continues, "I'd very much like to sit there and I have a coffee." I'm not sure what the coffee has to do with anything, but you learn when traveling to never dispute a grandma.

I'm reminded of the time I was queuing in Beijing to get through security to enter Tiananmen Square when I was sandwiched between two grandmas in front of me who weren't going to budge and two behind me who were simultaneously pushing me and using me to rest on. Another time, also in Beijing, a grandma noticed my bottle of soda was half finished, so she stood beside me waiting for me to finish so she could have my bottle to recycle. At least that's what I surmised as neither of us spoke the other's language.

In this instance, before I can even respond or move, she's started to work her way into my spot. There is a woman passing by whom, seeing my semi-confusion, mentions to the old lady that the seat next to me is vacant, but that's clearly not the spot she wants. The woman and I exchange a quick glance and she shrugs, wordlessly indicating, "What can you do?" In this case, and any case involving a grandma, absolutely nothing besides smile and get out of the way.

The Picky Eater

Puerto Rico – December 2019

My wife and I have recently gotten into food tours. Our first was earlier this year in Long Beach, following a conference I was attending. A few month later we were in Monterrey for another conference and located another food tour. The ones we have taken have been guided by locals and introduced not just food but regional history. As we've enjoyed them so far, we've decided to try to incorporate them into future travels.

So, we were very happy to have found one in San Juan, Puerto Rico. We're here for a few days before joining an Eastern Caribbean cruise. We've been to San Juan before, after my wife had moved over from London and couldn't travel internationally while her residency was being established. I proposed we head to Puerto Rico as she would only need her driver's license as identification. I don't think she completely believed me until we set foot on the island and no one tried to stop her.

Our tour is situated in old San Juan, just a few blocks from our hotel, and our guide is also a local yoga instructor. Our group is small and includes mostly people like us awaiting their Caribbean cruise departure. There's also another couple from Los Angeles—she's originally from Mexico and he doesn't appear to want to be there. He's wearing designer sunglasses and a tight t-shirt with Hugo Boss emblazoned in gold, which makes me assume he drives a Tesla back home.

Our first stop is a coffee shop that also serves scratch-made pastry. The assumed Tesla driver doesn't partake as he doesn't do gluten. We follow this stop with a walk about town, which is followed by a stop for freshly made fruit popsicles to quench the growing heat. These he passes on because he doesn't do sugar. A later stop includes white rice as a side but, you guessed it, he doesn't do white rice.

Now I can see why he didn't appear interested. I'm now assuming this food tour was his girlfriend's idea and she wouldn't let him head to the beach on his own as he might drown while trying to get out of the sea when he learns there's salt in it.

A Non-Inclusive Tour

St. Lucia – December 2019

Travel always has extra costs. Beyond flights and accommodations, there are extras such as transportation, meals, and admission fees to assorted attractions. Some tours include these, many do not. The best advice I've read regarding this said to set out all the clothes and money you have planned for a trip and then take half the clothes and twice the money. Wiser words have rarely been shared.

We're in Saint Lucia on Christmas day and I've booked a half-day private tour so that we can see a bit of the island without the guide needing to spend the whole day away from their family. As neither my wife nor I are beach people, it took some time to find an excursion that wasn't just lounging at a beach. Being a private tour, we're able to adjust some of what we see, though the sample itinerary provided pretty much covers what we'd like to see. It doesn't, though, cover extra costs.

We start with a visit to a roadside stand to sample some condiments and alcohol, all of which are available for sale. We purchase some banana ketchup and our guide tells us we'll be stopping by here on our way back to the port for lunch, which is $10 each. No problem, that beats a touristy restaurant in a busy part of town. We then head off for an elevated view of Marigot Bay, followed by an elevated view of Anse La Raye village and an elevated view of Canaries village. There are also several stops to view the island's famous twin pitons. At each stop there are sellers with assorted wares on display. Being Christmas, it seems wrong not to buy something, so my wife purchases a necklace.

Then the add-ons start. First up is La Soufriere Drive-In Volcano, where you can get an optional mud bath. We skip the mud path and opt for the view of the volcano, which is done with a local guide for an additional fee. Then it's Diamond Falls Botanical Gardens, which is done with a local guide for an additional fee (and don't forget the gift shop). Toraille Waterfall? No guide here, but there's an additional fee for the ticket that lets you in.

Good thing this is only a half-day tour as I'm not sure how much more I can contribute to the local economy at this rate. Officially the currency of Saint Lucia is the Eastern Caribbean dollar, but everyone accepts U.S. dollars, making my donations to the economy all that much easier. After our lunch we're back to the port and I make my final contribution to the local economy with a tip for our guide/driver. Now back to our cruise ship, where the food, and select beverages, are included.

Can't Get Here from There

California/China – February 2020

When my wife and I first met, she would go back to Beijing every year for Chinese New Year, as her grandmother, an aunt, two uncles, and two cousins still live in the area. As the new year occurs near the beginning of the spring term at my college, I'm not able to get away, so after one year going without me after we got married, we started going back to Beijing as part of our summer or winter travels every other year. We hadn't been back for a few years when her grandmother, now in her nineties, started hinting that it would be nice to see her, so she headed off on her own this year.

Of course, what we didn't know when planning this trip for her was the impact of the coronavirus, which originated in China. My wife would send me photos of typically packed streets near where her grandmother lives that were now vacant. It was both eerie and mesmerizing and made me wish I was there to witness it firsthand. Then the flights out of China started to be cancelled.

My wife's aunt and uncle who live in Israel cut their time in Beijing short as they weren't sure their originally scheduled flight would take off. It was a good call as the flight they switched to turned out to be the last one that airline would fly on that route. My wife and I keep an eye on the situation and the ever-changing dates her airline keeps giving for when they will start cancelling their flights out of China. When it looks like her flight home is most likely not going to happen, I start looking for alternatives.

When the cancellation notice comes, I've already booked her on another flight, this time with a Chinese airline. We both feel certain this one will be a go. We're coming up on the week she should be returning home when that flight is cancelled. I wake up to a frantic call from my wife who's been trying to reach her airline to find out her options, but the line has been overloaded and she's not been able to speak with anyone.

I find a U.S. number for the company, but it doesn't open for a few hours. I try to calm her while also seeing what our options are. Airlines are talking about not resuming flights until at least May and we're starting to wonder what we'd do in this case. The few remaining flights I can find are now extortionate in price and have no guarantee of not being cancelled.

I call the U.S. number as soon as it opens and expect to be on hold for a while, but within five minutes someone is on the line. I explain the situation to them and am informed in a matter-of-fact tone that my wife has already been booked on a flight leaving the next day, though the evening flight instead of the morning one. Why not put that in an email, I think, which would have saved us both a lot of distress. I ask for all of the details of the new flight and then call my wife back.

Still no guarantee this flight won't be cancelled as well, so we're both keeping our eyes on the airline's website and checking our email more than usual. Originally my wife was going to be arriving on Friday, so I took a personal day in order to pick her up. Now she's scheduled to arrive on Sunday, but I keep the personal day so I won't let the growing anxiety cloud my work. The flight leaves Beijing while I'm asleep, so I check my phone first thing to find texts from my wife as she is headed to the airport and when she is boarding the flight. It appears to all be a go, so I start tracking the flight online before heading out to LAX.

When I make it to the arrivals area of LAX's international terminal, I text my wife to let her know I've arrived, and she texts back to let me know she's landed. Then I don't hear from her for quite some time. Turns out neither the Centers for Disease Control and Prevention nor the Transportation Security Administration seem exactly sure what to do with arrivals, as they only began testing flights from China the day before. While my wife's temperature had been tested and she'd been surveyed upon arrival, when she gets to baggage claim, the security official is concerned as my wife hadn't been given anything proving this. So he has to call the person who screened my wife, who arrives fifteen minutes later to confirm he'd tested and surveyed her. Always good to see a system run smoothly.

Ironically, this was one year I could have gone back for the new year but didn't as I was saving my vacation days for trips in April and June. Those trips would soon be cancelled, and I'd be on the phone again arranging credits and refunds. Some airlines make this easy, while others do not, and it will be months until it is all settled. At least my wife is back home and we'll now be quarantining together rather than 6000 miles apart.

Made in the USA
Las Vegas, NV
28 January 2022

42481102R00066